A Second Chance

D1470398

A Second Chance

RICK HERRICK

RESOURCE *Publications* · Eugene, Oregon

A SECOND CHANCE

Copyright © 2022 Rick Herrick. All rights reserved. Except for brief quotations in critical publications or reviews, no part of this book may be reproduced in any manner without prior written permission from the publisher. Write: Permissions, Wipf and Stock Publishers, 199 W. 8th Ave., Suite 3, Eugene, OR 97401.

Resource Publications
An Imprint of Wipf and Stock Publishers
199 W. 8th Ave., Suite 3
Eugene, OR 97401

www.wipfandstock.com

PAPERBACK ISBN: 978-1-6667-3756-1
HARDCOVER ISBN: 978-1-6667-9713-8
EBOOK ISBN: 978-1-6667-9714-5

04/26/22

Scriptures taken from The Jerusalem Bible © 1966 by Darton Longman & Todd Ltd and Doubleday and Company Ltd.

To Jeff and Robert

Contents

Acknowledgements

THE FIRST VERSION OF *A Second Chance* came as a musical. Because of the prohibitive production costs of such a project and because of the slim prospects of acceptance, I turned the musical into a novel. Kate Hancock and Amy LaDeroute each suggested a scene for the musical based on their reading of an early draft. Those scenes became part of the novel, and for that I thank them.

Music for the original play was written by Ken LaDeroute. His spiritual songs and, even more impressive, the love and energy that flow so naturally from his healthy heart have inspired me over the many years of our friendship. The lyrics from two of his songs made their way into the novel.

Constructive criticism and generous encouragement were provided by Courtney and Ed Hand. My dear friend Les Woodcock helped me set the novel in New York City. Grammar and clarity were improved through the careful reading of Carol and Steve Humpherys. An early draft of the novel was read by my friend Deb Ward. When I asked her about the book, she smiled broadly, which told me all was well.

Acknowledgements

The book is dedicated to two of Lyn's and my oldest friends. Jeff Lakeman and Robert Delano have kept us laughing for forty years. Their creative lives have inspired us. Thank you both for being such loyal friends.

Finally, I want to thank the Wipf and Stock staff for their friendly cooperation in putting this project together and their considerable help with editing the final draft.

1

Rapture Ready

DR. GEORGE SAUNDERS WAS sitting in the den of their apartment on 400 Riverside Drive watching the local news. All the talk was about Andrew Cuomo's recent resignation as governor of New York and the fall of Afghanistan to the Taliban. Although George wasn't sure what he thought about Cuomo's resignation, he was sure about his concern for the hospital. The delta virus was surging, and hospital space was again becoming a premium. He worried about whether they would force him to stop performing elective surgery. George was an attending general surgeon at Columbia Presbyterian Hospital.

His partner of twenty years, Jonathan Thurman, better known to his friends as Queenie, was sitting in the corner of the den quietly strumming his guitar. He was writing a song about an old friend who had died from the COVID-19 virus six months before. His focus was interrupted by a text on his cell phone.

"George. Greg just texted me. A group of our friends is meeting at Central Park to decide on a place for dinner. I was planning on leftovers here. Let's go."

"Fine with me. I've had it with the news." They left their seventeen-hundred-square-foot apartment that fronted the Hudson

River for the ten-minute walk to Central Park as soon as George was able to replace his blue scrubs with more casual attire.

The Reverend Dr. Julian Norcross, pastor of Stillwater Baptist Church on West Fifty-Seventh Street, a graduate of Liberty University and the Southern Baptist Theological Seminary in Louisville, Kentucky, was enjoying an early dinner with his wife, Brianna, when the telephone rang. After speaking on the phone briefly, he looked across at his wife and said, "It's Rev. Smithfield. The Rapture Ready Index has risen above 160, which makes it 'fasten your seatbelt' time."

"Oh, Julian," Brianna said. "The Lord is returning. This is so exciting."

"I want as many of our members to witness it as possible."

"What do you think pushed the index over the top?"

"I'm betting the raging fires in California or maybe the recent fall of Afghanistan to the Satan-infested Taliban. But the point is Christ is returning. Call Dorothy. Have her email all church members, informing them that the second coming is here. We will meet in the southwest corner of Central Park as soon as it's possible for people to get there. There is no better place to watch our Jesus return on the clouds of heaven." While Brianna made the call, Rev. Norcross wolfed down the rest of his dinner and waited impatiently for his wife. They left for the fifteen-minute walk to Central Park at 6:15 p.m.

Jesus was indeed returning. He had left Jerusalem the night before on an American Airlines flight to JFK. The flight landed at 3:50 in the afternoon on Sunday, August 15, 2021. He was here on a small grant from the Historical Society of Israel.

After deplaning and making it through customs, he proceeded to the travel-information booth in the baggage-claim area. There, he asked the middle-aged African American woman at the desk to help with an Uber reservation. He ended up handing her his cell phone and allowing her to make the reservation. The Historical Society had given him the cell phone and a Visa credit card with a five-thousand-dollar balance.

"Your driver's name is Dima," the woman reported with a warm smile. "He will arrive in twelve minutes. Just exit through the sliding glass doors and walk about a hundred yards to your left. He will be driving a blue Honda CR-V."

"Thank you so much," Jesus said. "That's the first time I have used this phone," he said, smiling at her as he stepped away from the booth.

"Good luck," the woman said before turning her attention to the next person in line. Jesus proceeded to the meeting place, and Dima was right on time.

"Times Square?" Dima asked as he eased the car from the curb.

"I can't wait," Jesus said. "I've heard so much about it in Israel."

"It should take about thirty-five minutes," Dima said, "depending on traffic. You won't be disappointed. There is so much to see there."

"You have an interesting accent," Jesus said. "Where are you from?"

"Russia originally. I came here twenty-five years ago."

"What brought you here?"

"I had just graduated from university and was celebrating with friends who were drinking vodka. I got drunk and, in that state, made the decision to fly to New York. One of my drunken buddies came with me. He eventually returned to Moscow, and I married an American lady."

"An interesting story. Do you live in the city?"

"No, we live in Hoboken, New Jersey—Frank Sinatra's hometown. Have you heard of Sinatra?"

"I don't think so."

"One of the great American singers from the forties and fifties."

"I'd like to hear him. How long have you lived there?"

"Since we were first married in 1999. My wife owns a restaurant there."

"Has COVID been hard on your business?"

"Brutal. We don't do takeout, so we've been closed for almost a year. That's why I'm driving for Uber. I don't know what we would have done without the government stimulus programs."

"Do you work at the restaurant?"

"Yes, I'm the fill-in guy. Some nights I seat customers, sometimes I wait table. I even do dishes whenever we have a no-show."

"Does the restaurant specialize in terms of the food you serve?"

"No, we have a rather generic menu for both lunch and dinner. My wife says the key to success is good food, reasonable prices, and a fun atmosphere. She works hard at making the restaurant fun. We have live entertainment most nights."

"Sounds like you're doing really well."

"We were, and we will avoid bankruptcy. We're just starting up again. I have crossed fingers. Tell me a little about yourself. You have on an interesting costume."

"My name is Jesus, and I was born and raised in Nazareth in Galilee."

"Are you shittin' me, man?" Dima asked as he looked at Jesus through the rearview mirror with a puzzled look on his face.

"No, it's me. I've come back."

"Wow—too much. I can't believe it. My wife will think I've been eating the wrong kind of mushrooms when I tell her."

"There's nothing to believe. Here I am."

"Wow again. Even if you're not the real thing, I'd love to see you again. Here's my card." And he reached into the back seat to hand Jesus his card. "We'd love to have you at the restaurant for a 'Welcome Back, Jesus' night."

"I'd be happy to consider it, Dima. Are you Russian Orthodox?"

"I come from that tradition. Most Russians do."

"I know. I bet you have no idea why you come from that tradition."

"I was taught as a kid it was the one true faith."

"Let me tell you a story. You can test that assumption against this story. The story of how Russia adopted Orthodox Christianity begins in the tenth century. Grand Prince Vladimir I was a pagan with a consuming ambition to unify the Russian tribes into a single nation. He considered several possible approaches to integrating the state, and eventually decided the best way to achieve his goal was to use religion.

"He sent out special emissaries to explore three possibilities. The first was Roman Catholicism. Although there were no doctrinal issues that concerned him, he concluded it would be dangerous to subject his country to the political intrigues and power struggles of Western Europe. He also looked into Islam and rejected it for similar reasons. Actually, this process of deliberation was more pretense than real, because conversion to the Greek Orthodox faith would enable him to marry the beautiful sister of the emperor of Constantinople, whom he coveted.

"In 988, Vladimir herded all citizens of Kiev at knife point to the Dnieper River to be baptized into the Orthodox faith. One man's desire for a woman decided the religious fate of an entire nation. Over the years, Russian Orthodox Christians came to believe that only they practiced religion in a manner acceptable to God. This claim is a remarkable one, considering the fact these people could have become Muslims if the Muslim ruler during Vladimir's search had had a beautiful daughter."

"Good story, Jesus, but you may be wrong about Vladimir's decision."

"How so?"

"I think he chose the Greek Orthodox lady because no one told him if he went Muslim he could have more than one wife."

"You may be right about that," Jesus responded with a smile. "How would you have done with a name like Muhammad?"

"I expect I would have gotten used to it."

"Good for you. Christianity or Islam is not the important thing. What matters most is loving your neighbor."

"I try to do that. Now, listen. We're almost there. Where are you staying tonight? I'd be happy to make a recommendation."

"Thanks, but I'm all set. I'm staying at the Appalachian State University loft on East Twenty-Fourth Street. Two months ago, I met an archeology professor from that university on a dig in the tiny village of Magdala on the Sea of Galilee. He was studying the fish-salting industry in the first century, and I was looking for any remains from the home of my great friend Mary. The professor and I became good friends, and he made the arrangements. When I left, he assured me it would be at least three months before the research team got near the first century."

"You're all set, then," Dima said as he pulled his car up to the curb of a sidewalk in front of the Knickerbocker Hotel. "Do you see the street sign for Broadway on the corner? In a block, Broadway becomes a pedestrian walkway. Just follow Broadway, and it will take you right to Times Square—no more than ten minutes from here."

"Thank you, Dima. It was a very pleasant trip," Jesus said as he moved two steps to Dima's front-seat window. He reached into his pocket for a five-dollar bill. "Here's a tip for your good work. My professor friend coached me that this was a good thing to do in these circumstances."

"No thanks, Jesus. The pleasure was all mine. And please think about coming to our restaurant. You've got my card. Bring your friends. The meal will be on us."

"I'll remember, Dima. Just up Broadway. You left me at a good place."

"Have fun," Dima said as he smiled at Jesus. "I've got to run. I have a pickup in ten minutes at Grand Central Station." Jesus walked behind the car, removed his protective mask, and headed up Broadway, traveling light with a haversack and staff. It was an exciting jaunt with crowds of people, neon signs, and tall buildings. He stopped frequently to people watch. He was fascinated to see such a variety of people and costumes.

But nothing prepared him for the man in his underwear and cowboy hat playing his red, white, and blue guitar. He's not great on the guitar, Jesus concluded, but maybe he's a real cowboy? He had heard a lot about them, a breed of humanity uniquely American, but was this how they dressed? He needed a tour guide.

As he was staring at the cowboy, two men dressed in tunics similar to his own passed by carrying "Free Tibet" signs. "Amen," Jesus said, smiling over at them. He was a Dalai Lama fan. He continued walking north on Broadway, carefully dodging the crowd moving in the opposite direction. It didn't take long, however, before he was staring again. Two topless women with painted breasts were approaching him. "Oh my," he mumbled to himself. "I've arrived on a different planet." His heart missed a beat when the woman with breasts painted in red stopped to admire his tunic.

"I like the simple gray, but you could make a much bigger splash if you cut away the seat of your pants. You could moon the city of New York."

"I better not do that," Jesus responded sheepishly. "I only have one additional tunic in my sack to replace it. But I do have a question for you."

"Shoot, brother. I'm all ears. It's a nice change. For most people around here, I'm all tits and ass."

"Have I arrived at Times Square? It must be nearby from the directions I received."

"Look over your shoulder to the left. Do you see the Hard Rock Café? That says you are right in the middle of things."

"Can I get a drink of water there? I must admit to being a little parched."

"They've got a lot more than water there."

"Great. I think I'll try it," he said, smiling and trying to keep his eyes focused above her shoulders.

"You're going to get a stiff neck if you keep looking at me like that. Enjoy my floppies. Just no touchy."

"You don't have to worry about that," Jesus said as he quickly turned left to walk the few steps to the café. "Thanks again for setting me straight about Times Square."

"I guess there are no tips from weirdos dressed in tunics," the woman grumbled to herself as she hurried to catch up with her bouncing partner.

In his hurry to leave the red-breasted woman, Jesus bumped into a middle-aged man wearing a "Fuck the Police" T-shirt.

"Go back to your homeless shelter, asshole," the man yelled at Jesus.

Shaken, Jesus landed up against an outside table at the Hard Rock Café with four young women in their twenties seated there, laughing, with drinks in hand.

"Hi, cutie. You look lost," the woman with the sandy blond hair on the chair to the right said.

Jesus, regaining his balance and some semblance of composure, mumbled to himself, laughing: "Here I am supposed to be the good shepherd, but this woman is right. I'm the one that's lost." He smiled over at her and said, "Your city is a little overwhelming."

"Come join us for a drink," said a second woman with short, dark-brown hair who was directly opposite from Jesus.

"It will feel good to sit," Jesus said as he pulled up a chair from an adjacent table. "A little water would hit the spot."

"Change that order to wine, Monica," the woman on the left, who had bright red hair, said. "This dude needs a pick-me-up." The woman sitting to Jesus' right poured him a glass of red wine from the bottle at the table.

"I did that once."

"You did what?" The redhead asked with a warm smile.

"Oh, the wine thing," Jesus responded. After pausing briefly, Jesus looked across at the woman with the long, sandy blond hair and asked, "Do you women work in the city?"

"That we do," the sandy blond responded, "but this isn't about work. It's girl time and boy talk."

"My boyfriend and I are trying to decide whether to try a threesome," the redhead said. "But you wouldn't know anything about that."

"Some people say I'm part of a threesome, but that's a really silly idea."

"Who did you say you are? We need to be formally introduced," the woman sitting to his left said.

"I'm Jesus from Nazareth."

"Nice to meet you, Jesus. I'll start with the redhead on your left. That's Brittany. The one across from you with the short, dark hair is Monica. Sitting beside her is Holly, and I'm Paige."

"Nice to meet you all."

"He'd be perfect, Monica," Holly spoke quietly to her friend. "Why not ask him to be your number three? He's probably pretty horny after two thousand years of celibate life."

"At one point in the Bible, I think he even talks about being 'in me and I in you.' Sounds like a threesome to me. I like his trim beard, the shoulder-length brown hair, and those dark-brown eyes are penetrating. You may be right. He also looks about our age—maybe a little older."

"What's all this talk about?" Jesus asked with a smile.

"Oh, my friends are just babbling incoherently," Paige replied. "What led you to return to earth?"

"I came back because there are some things about my message that need correcting. I'm looking for a messenger. Would any of you be interested?"

"Say yes, Monica," Holly said. "The guys would think you're hot."

"While we're waiting with baited breath to hear Monica's reply, have some of my fries, Jesus," Brittany said. "I have a figure to protect." Jesus smiled at her and took her up on the offer.

"These are good," he said with a smile. "I've never had anything like this before. They have a rather strange potato-like taste."

"They're called french fries, but I have no idea what the French had to do with it," Brittany said.

"They may have been the first to cut potatoes into thin slices," Jesus replied.

"You're good, Jesus. That's the best explanation I've ever heard."

"No, Monica. As Mark says in his Gospel, only God is good."

"What does Mark know, anyway?" Holly said.

"I often agree with you, Holly, especially when I read Mark's claim that I was the Son of Man."

"Who's that?" Monica asked.

"Some guy who sits in heaven with God and returns to earth at the end of history on the clouds of heaven to rescue the righteous and take them to heaven. Do I look like I came from the clouds of heaven?"

"You look pretty earthy to me in that cute gray tunic," Holly replied.

"Who made up such a story?" Paige asked.

"The prophet Daniel."

"The guy in the lion's den?" Brittany asked.

"He's the one."

"Too bad the lions didn't get him," Brittany said.

"I know exactly what happened. That story somehow found its way into the internet cloud," Holly said. "That internet cloud is a cloud in heaven, as far as I'm concerned."

"What's this internet cloud?" Jesus asked.

"That's where crazy stories go that end up being broadcast all over the world," Holly replied.

"You're the one who's good, Holly. Are you sure you wouldn't consider being my messenger?"

"No. I'm afraid you'd find I'm not very good in front of people. Why not ask Trump? He's currently without a job, and he's good at spreading false stories."

"He'd be perfect," Monica said. "Tell him he is God's Son of Man. He'd love it. He can come down from heaven in his golf cart and take all the anti-vaxxers to heaven. You could end the pandemic, Jesus."

"Listen up, everyone," Brittany said. "It's Ricky Nelson's 'Garden Party,' one of my favorite songs. My mom used to play it all the time." There was a pause in the conversation which was interrupted when Brittany joined Ricky with the chorus: "I learned my lesson well. You see, you can't please everyone. So you got to please yourself."

"Don't forget your neighbor. That's part of my message." And then, after a brief pause, Jesus continued. "He's got a nice voice. Maybe he could be my messenger."

"Sadly, he died in a plane crash," Brittany said. "I think it happened before we were born."

"You ladies aren't much help with my messenger," Jesus said with a smile.

"Oh look, Jesus. Robin Red Breasts is back," Holly said.

"What a strange costume. Who are these two?"

"They're called 'desnudas,' whatever that means," Holly said. "It's best to stay away from them. They're only after your money."

"Where do you put it?" Jesus inquired. "They have no pockets."

"You stuff it in their panties," Monica said.

"There's not much room in those tiny things," Jesus replied.

"They only take paper money," Brittany said.

"Then I better save my silver denarius for someone more fully clothed."

"Smart man," Brittany responded. "Don't buy any theater tickets on the street either. They're panhandlers too. The tickets are no good. They're just after your money."

"Thanks for all of that good advice," Jesus said, "and for the good wine and french fries. I better be on my way so I'm not late for my reservation at the loft, but I want to see Central Park first. Can you give me directions?"

"Just stay on Broadway," Brittany said. "It's two or three blocks from here. A ten-minute walk—no more."

Jesus got up from his chair, smiled at his new friends, and handed them his card. "In case any of you change your mind about being my messenger, here's my card. It would be an honor if one of you was willing to help me." He smiled at them one last time and continued his walk up Broadway.

Twenty minutes later, Jesus crossed Fifty-Ninth Street and entered the park in the southwest corner at Columbus Circle. After spending a few minutes taking in the well-manicured grass and the assortment of trees scattered throughout, he spotted a group of a hundred or more people looking toward heaven. His curiosity caused him to inexorably move toward them. A short, barrel-chested man at the head of the group raised his arms up high and spoke out in a clear, though somewhat-stilted, voice: "Take us, Jesus. We are ready to meet you in the air."

A man from the crowd called out: "The fall of Afghanistan has revealed the Arab beast. Satan has been uncovered, the dirty Taliban terrorists exposed. Lead your saints to establish the one-thousand-year kingdom. We are ready."

Another called out: "Amen, brother. Throw Satan into the burning lake. We are ready, Jesus."

He was followed by a woman in the group: "Sweet Jesus, lead your heavenly armies to defeat the beast and destroy Babylon. We are ready."

Jesus wandered into the crowd and said to no one in particular, "I'm glad to know someone thinks of me as sweet, but why are you all looking up at the sky? Is that Venus you see up there?"

The short, barrel-chested man yelled out: "We are looking for Jesus. The rapture is here. Do you believe?"

"I have arrived."

"I see you are here," the man replied. "Let me baptize you this instant so you, too, can be saved."

"What, in that bird bath over there?"

"This is no time for jokes," the barrel-chested man replied. "The time is now. God's promises will be fulfilled. Our Holy Scriptures validated. Have you read our Holy Scriptures?"

"Some people claim I wrote them," Jesus responded.

"Who is this nutcase?" a man shouted out from the crowd.

"Yes, my friend. Be careful what you say about our sacred Scriptures. Blasphemers will soon burn. My name is Dr. Julian Norcross, pastor of Stillwater Baptist Church."

Jesus extended his hand to the man and said, "Nice to meet you, Julian. I am Jesus, born and raised in Nazareth. We didn't have any streets in the first century. Just a lot of walking paths."

Another man from the crowd shouted out, "This guy is obviously an imposter. The Son of God was born in Bethlehem. His mother was a perpetual virgin."

"Did you tell my dad that? He might not agree with you on that point."

"I don't know who you are or what you are doing here," Dr. Norcross said.

"I'm looking for a messenger, someone to tell the world it can have a second chance."

"There is no second chance," Dr. Norcross rebutted. "The rapture is here. Repent and come to our Lord."

"I'm here to say there will be no rapture. It's all about loving your neighbor in this world, about bringing God's kingdom to earth, about making the world a better place."

"What right do you have to tell us anything? You're crazier than a loon," Dr. Norcross called out.

"I guess I'll have to go elsewhere. Maybe those guys over there to the left will be more receptive."

"You may have a point there. Those guys you are pointing at are all queerer than a three-dollar bill and will be the first to burn. I tell you most truly, our heavenly Father hates their sin."

"What do you mean by queerer? Are you saying they're different?"

"I'm saying they are gay."

"Oh, that means they're happy. Good for them."

"I'm saying they do it man to man."

"Do what?"

"Shoot blanks, you dumb ass," a man shouted from the crowd.

"My brothers and sisters, we must end this nonsense with this silly imposter. Kind sir, please leave us immediately and join those queers as I was just saying. They'll think you're cute in that dress." And the congregation broke out in cheers and loud catcalls.

"Thanks for your time. I may check with you later to see how this rapture thing works out." Jesus left the rapture-ready believers and walked fifty yards along a narrow gravel path to join a collection of eight guys in animated discussion. "Hi there," Jesus said, as he extended his hand to George. "I'm Jesus. And you are?"

"Nice to meet you, Jesus," George replied, shaking the outstretched hand. "My name is Judas. We go back a long way. I apologize for screwing you two thousand years ago; however, if you bend over, I'd be happy to do it again."

"George, come on," Jonathan said. "Take it easy on this guy. He looks like he comes from Queens."

"No, I'm the guy from Nazareth."

"And what, may I ask, brought you to our little circle of friends?" Greg Shapiro asked. Greg was a vice president at Morgan Stanley and the partner of Brad Bridges, a senior accountant at Ernst and Young. They shared a luxury apartment on the corner of Broadway and Murray Street.

"I'm looking for a messenger to help me correct some of the many mistakes in the New Testament. One of them concerns the rapture. That group over there is obsessed with that crazy idea."

"Where does it come from?" Greg asked.

"The term comes from Paul's Letter to the Thessalonians. Some early Christians believed that at the end of time, they would rise to meet me in the air. From there, I would take them to heaven. They've waited two thousand years for this event to take place, and I'm afraid there is a lot more waiting to do."

"Sounds like a nice trip. My friends and I would love to relocate those bigots in heaven. With regard to your messenger, you might have better luck next door." And Greg pointed in the direction of Rev. Norcross's group, where most eyes had regained their focus on heaven.

"I just came from over there. They sent me to you guys."

"And you came?" Brad said. "We keep hearing from people like them that homosexuality is a sin."

"That's a part of the story I want to correct. The apostle Paul had many nice things to say, but he also made mistakes. He never spoke for me when, in his Letter to the Romans, he called homosexuality an 'abomination.'"

"A Jesus who likes gays," George said. "I wonder how many incarnations it took God to come up with that result?"

"Very few people I knew in the first century were concerned about homosexuality. The Greeks and Romans practiced it widely. Sexual orientation has nothing to do with religion, as far as I'm concerned."

George's cell phone rang, and he looked across at Jonathan. "Queenie, I may be headed back to the hospital. I better take this call over here away from you all." And he moved away from the group.

Greg continued the conversation with Jesus. "Why did you decide to come back now?"

"Because Christians are hung up on salvation. The point of my teachings was to live with love here on earth, now. Who knows what happens at the end of life?"

"Interesting," Brad responded. "Tell me about your credentials?"

"I don't have many. I just learned to read a few years ago."

"Let's get back to your looking for a messenger," Greg said. "Why not ask someone like Cardinal Dolan? He's right here in the city."

"Because he's part of the problem. Millions of Christians like him have sanitized me, taken me right out of history. I'm the nice guy who loves you, forgives you, and takes you to heaven. They are deliriously happy to live in salvation la-la land while the rest of the world suffers from poverty and the ravages of climate change. Of course, I love people and forgive them, but I was never interested in sin and salvation in heaven. My message was about establishing God's kingdom on earth, about organizing society around God's love, about building a world that is nonviolent, inclusive, with a passionate concern for economic and social justice."

"Sounds nice to me, Jesus," Brad responded. "Good luck."

George moved back to the group and spoke to Jonathan. "Queenie, I do have to go back to the hospital. An older patient of mine has a raging septic infection throughout her body."

"What prospects does a woman like that have?" Greg asked.

"If the antibiotics don't get the infection under control, her prospects aren't good," George replied as he moved toward Jesus.

"Nice to meet you, Jesus. We need to continue this conversation. Queenie and I are having a party this coming Saturday. Please join us. Queenie can give you directions," George said, smiling over at Jesus. "Later, guys." And he moved toward the park entrance with haste.

As George disappeared around the corner, Jonathan spoke further with Jesus. "My friends call me Queenie, but my real name is Jonathan. I didn't want you to become confused."

"Nice to meet you, Jonathan. You have a nice group of friends."

"They are a good group. I also wanted to apologize for George's rather crude joke about Judas. He didn't mean any disrespect."

"I didn't take it that way. The plain truth is, the joke went right over my head."

"That's good. Can we entice you to join us for dinner? We're getting ready to head for Times Square right now."

"I better say no to your kind offer. I have to check in at the loft where I'm staying in a little more than an hour. However, I would love to come to your party. I feel good about the prospect of finding a messenger from among you. Here is my card. You can call my cell phone with the party details on Friday."

"I'll do it. We would love to have you. Good luck finding your hotel, and I'll call Friday morning." Jonathan patted Jesus on the shoulder and left to rejoin his friends.

2

Ms. Rip Van Winkle

AMY FITZGERALD, A NURSE in the intensive care unit at Columbia Presbyterian Hospital, entered the room of Grace Bowdoin, who was suffering from a raging septic infection following a routine gall bladder operation. Grace was intubated and receiving medicine intravenously. Amy was fully masked and washed her hands before moving to Grace's bed to check her vital signs. As she recorded her findings in the computer, the respiratory therapist, Tonya Kelly, also fully masked, entered the room. Tonya smiled at Amy as she checked Grace's vitals.

"You said Dr. Saunders is coming in to check on this patient?" Tonya asked while looking across at Amy. "I'm increasing her antibiotics. This is looking very dangerous to me."

"I called him half an hour ago. Her blood pressure is really low, and her white blood cell count is rising. He was worried about her when he left the hospital after rounds."

"We may lose her if things don't stabilize quickly," Tonya said. "It's a good thing this isn't Florida or Texas. At least we have a respirator for her."

"It would be really sad if we lost her," Amy said. "Her husband is a precious man. Have you met him?"

"Not really to talk to. I've seen him a few times in the room."

"He went home to call their kids. Dr. Saunders explained the seriousness of the situation to him this afternoon."

"She's lucky. He's a good doctor," Tonya said.

"Conscientious too," Amy replied.

After a brief pause, Tonya continued. "Well, Benjamin's Little League season is finally over. I'm going to miss the games. It's a major part of my social life."

"Do you watch the games with your ex?" Amy asked, smiling across at her friend. They had worked together in this unit of the hospital for the last seven years. "Those situations can get awkward."

"Dan and I have no problems together. We can be quite civil when it benefits the kids, although, as you know, we are far from being friends."

"How's the emailing going with Match.com?"

"I'm corresponding with three guys," Tonya said. "I'm ready to have coffee with one of them."

"What's the process like? It seems a little scary to me."

"Well, it certainly beats the bar scene. Actually, it's not really scary, just time-consuming. You begin with emails. Then you talk on the phone. Eventually, you meet at some neutral place for a coffee or something similar. That's the way I do it, anyway."

"That first meeting must be something."

"It's different. The last time I met someone, it was a disaster. Well, not quite a disaster, but a definite no go. I knew almost immediately."

"What happened? This is so out of my league."

"It looked really good over the phone. He's a physical therapist at the rehab hospital in Queens. So we had something in common. He sounded really nice on the phone, but when we met at Starbucks—whoa. He was huge. Not like his picture at all. His ass just spread out all across the chair."

"Sounds like my kinda guy," George said as he entered the room fully masked.

"Oh, hi, Dr. Saunders," Tonya said, giggling. "You made good time getting here."

George moved directly to Grace's bed. He looked at her tenderly, checked her pulse, and gently squeezed her hand. "Keep on fighting, Grace. You're a beautiful woman. I'd hate to lose you." He then went to check the ventilator settings and read through her chart. "You were smart to up her antibiotics, Tonya."

"I just did that before you came in."

"I don't like what I'm seeing here," George said as he wrote some notes on Grace's chart. "Don't hesitate to call me again if her situation worsens."

"I won't, Dr. Saunders," Amy responded.

"She's in good hands. If she makes it through tonight, she has a chance," George said, smiling across at the two ladies before exiting the room.

It was 2:00 a.m. on Thursday morning. Grace remained intubated and in a sleeping coma in her bed in the ICU unit at Columbia Presbyterian. Her husband, Keith, sat alongside her bed watching Amy change the dressing to her wound. "Am I going to lose her?"

"She's an amazing woman, Keith. Something is keeping her here," Amy said as she finished her work and moved away from Grace's bed. Keith pushed his chair closer to the bed so he could take her hand.

"Well, all the kids are here. If we have to lose her, the important people have said their goodbyes." Tears formed around Keith's tired eyes. Amy patted him on the shoulder before taking a seat at the head of Grace's bed.

"I've seen a lot of remarkable recoveries in this room. We haven't given up yet."

"That's good. She's the best thing that has ever happened to me. We've been married for fifty-five years. We met on a blind date at fifteen."

"Was it love at first sight?"

"It was for me. I think it took Gracey a few years to catch up."

"What's the secret to making a beautiful marriage like yours work?"

"There may not be one answer that fits all, but in our case, the explanation is simple. We both wanted to be our own person, to live authentic lives. The key for us is that neither one sought to control the other. We gave each other lots of space and took pride in the results of our respective journeys."

"That sounds so nice. My marriage is all about coping—young kids, bills to pay, demanding schedules to juggle."

"That's your age. We went through that too. Just create some time for you and your husband together. You need that time, and your kids need a break from you."

"We try to go out on a date one night a week."

"Perfect," Keith said as he smiled across at her. "One day you'll look back fondly on this phase of your life. You may not want to go back to it, but you will be proud of what you have achieved—healthy kids, some financial stability, a marriage that is loving and has some depth." Keith paused in his conversation with Amy, released Grace's hand, and lovingly stroked her face and hair. "She's still a beautiful woman, even at less than a hundred pounds."

"She is that. A strong one too. What gives her all this strength?"

"She walks every day with three other women. You've met two of them—Ginger and Julie. They typically walk for an hour or more. She has good eating habits too. She works hard at keeping her weight down."

"Oh, hi, Dr. Saunders," Amy said with a note of surprise. "You're here early."

"I had an exploratory laparotomy," he said as he moved toward Grace's bed to examine her. "Not much change here." And then he smiled at Keith and patted him on the shoulder. "She's a beautiful woman, Keith."

"We were just talking about that, Dr. Saunders. What are her chances? Am I going to lose her?"

"I wish I could answer that. Keep holding her hand. There's mystery in the healing process."

"Do you believe in miracles?" Keith asked with a sheepish grin.

"I can't answer that either. I'm a scientist, and yet surprising things happen. Amy can certainly testify to that."

"You're on tonight, Dr. Saunders. We were talking about that too," Amy said with a wide grin.

"Sometimes you get lucky in the middle of the night."

"I know you're exhausted, Dr. Saunders. Whatever happens, I want you to know how much we appreciate what you have done for us. You're a great doctor with a big heart."

"That's really nice, Keith. You know, for me, this is just a job, and yet some of my patients, like your Grace, really tug at me." After smiling at Keith, he turned to Amy. "I'll be spending the rest of the night down the hall. Don't hesitate to wake me if her condition changes. When was her last chest X-ray?"

"This morning around ten."

"Let's see if we can get her another one soon. You take care Keith, and get some sleep yourself. This is your doctor speaking." George laughed, smiled at Amy, and left the room.

"What's the X-ray for?"

"We periodically check for pneumonia. It's routine. There's nothing to worry about, but I better get to it. I'll be back soon. In the meantime, you have your doctor's orders." Amy smiled across at Keith before leaving the room to find an X-ray technician.

Tonya removed the ventilator from Grace's room late Friday afternoon. Amy smiled as she watched from outside the room. When Tonya was finished, Amy entered the room and said, "Ms. Rip Van Winkle. Welcome back. It's been a long week."

"Who is Ms. Rip Van Winkle?" Grace asked, a little disoriented and blinking her eyes to adjust to the bright lights.

"You are," Amy said with a smile. "Your husband gave you the nickname. He was convinced you would wake up."

"Bless him. Where is Keith?"

"Sound asleep in the visitors' waiting room. He spent a lot of time in there while you slept here."

"He's a precious man. And you must be my nurse?"

"Yes, I'm Amy. You gave us quite a scare, Mrs. Bowdoin."

"Grace, please. I just remember being so very sick."

"Gallbladder disease can make you feel that way. The real problem was the septic infection."

"You're kidding."

"The infection was raging, but we seem to finally have it under control."

"That's good. Thank you all so much."

"How do you feel?"

"A little woozy, but I have no pain."

"That's a good sign there's no pain. I should probably check your vitals again," Amy said. She performed this with dispatch and then proceeded to the computer to enter the data. "Everything looks good."

"My, this is some news. Have the kids been here?"

"Yes, all four of them. Grandkids too. They're a good-looking group."

"This really was serious."

"Yes, it was, and you're not quite out of the woods yet. But things look so much better."

"Are the kids still here?"

"Yes, and I expect them sometime later this afternoon."

As Amy was speaking, Dr. Saunders arrived at the entrance to the room and began reading through Grace's data on the clipboard. He entered the room, smiled at the two women, and said, "You gave us a real scare Grace, but your blood pressure has stabilized and your white blood cell count is trending down. You have been given 'a second chance,' Mrs. Bowdoin," George called out with enthusiasm.

"Thank you, Dr. Saunders. I'm beginning to think I owe you my life."

"I was part of a good team. Amy watched you carefully and kept me informed about the ups and downs of your condition. Tonya, did you meet her?"

"I don't think so, Doctor."

"Well, she monitored your ventilator with great skill. Most important, your husband held your hand," George said as he looked around the room for Keith. "Where is Keith, anyway?"

"Asleep in the visitors' lounge."

"Good for him. He's earned it," George said as he looked across at Amy. "I'd like to keep her here one more day so you can keep an eye on her. If she continues to remain stable, we'll transfer her to a regular floor tomorrow." George then moved to Grace's bed, took her hand, looked closely at her, smiled, and said, "All we need from you, Grace, is a good fart."

"Excuse me, Doctor?" Grace replied, somewhat embarrassed.

"That tells us your bowel function has returned and we can start feeding you," Amy interpreted.

"Oh. Maybe I better try that while Keith is still asleep."

"Wait for your grandkids. They'll love it," George said, laughing. "Actually, anytime will be fine," he said while releasing Grace's hand. "You take care, and I'll check again before I leave for the night."

3

Party Time

THE APARTMENT OF GEORGE and Jonathan on Riverside Drive was party central for a rather large group of twenty or more friends. They had a routine. Guests brought a dish and a bottle of wine. Jonathan set up a bar at one end of the living room, and the food, along with plates and silverware, was placed on the dining room table. When Jonathan was satisfied that all was in order, he joined a group of partygoers in deep discussion of the tragedy unfolding in Afghanistan.

"Biden's going to take some shit on this one," said Sam, one of the more conservative members of the group. He was an economics professor at NYU. "It may even be somewhat deserved, even though our carrot-topped friend made an agreement to leave even earlier."

"I think the current tempest will blow over quickly," Stuart, a bankruptcy lawyer, said. "The speed of the collapse was breathtaking. It really proves Biden's point."

"It's shameful the Afghan troops were not willing to defend their wives, their daughters, their sisters, and all the other women in their lives," Rebecca said. Rebecca was a high school history teacher and the wife of Ron, an architect and former partner of Jonathan. "We lavished all this money on them, gave them the best weapons, and trained them for twenty years, and they ran."

"Afghanistan politicians ran with them," Stuart interjected.

"A little more advanced planning would have been helpful," Sam said.

"I love you, buddy, but no one in Washington—and I mean no one—expected the immediate collapse of a three-hundred-thousand-man military," Larry said. Larry was Sam's partner and a trial lawyer in the public defender's office.

"Hey, lighten up, everyone," George said as he joined the discussion. "This is party time. Let me tell you about this friend of mine at the hospital who's a urologist. I met him in the cafeteria the other day, and he broke out laughing. He had just given this man in his office a routine prostate exam. When the guy bent over, Ollie looked down and the guy had a target painted on his ass."

"That's a good idea," David said. "I'll have that done next time I go on a blind date."

"I can lighten things up a bit too," Rebecca said. "I was giving a test this spring, and I caught this kid texting. When I first noticed it from the perspective of my desk, it looked like he was playing with himself. I was shocked and confused as to what to do. He had both hands under the desk, and they were moving rapidly. I expected an explosion any minute."

"Was he smiling?" Sam asked.

"No, but I was smiling with relief when I realized he was actually texting, and went over to take his phone."

Smiling himself, Jonathan moved on to another section of the living room and joined a deep discussion about the rapture. He listened for a minute or two and went to their bedroom to get his guitar. He took a chair to the cedar chest, stepped up on it, and then stepped onto the chest, using it as a seat.

"Hey, folks. Brian, Don, and Greg are over in the corner having a deep discussion about the rapture, and I have an announcement to make. Jesus is actually coming here tonight. I spoke with him on the phone yesterday, and he promised to join us. I do want to play one song for you. It's about our dear friend Alex, who we lost to COVID. Let me know what you think." After finishing the song, Jonathan drifted off, improvising background music.

Greg soon took center stage. "Okay, boys and girls. Time to play Interpret that Scripture."

George shouted, "What's this shit?"

A few others called out, "We want Queenie. We want Queenie."

"You just had Queenie," Greg responded.

"No, I had Queenie," George called out with a laugh.

"I'm not going to compete with that," Greg said, "but we are going to play this game. I've spent the last three days researching it. Here's how it goes. I recite a scripture, and you shout out your interpretation. We're doing this to honor our Christian brothers we met at the park last Monday, who we hope will be leaving us soon as they travel with Jesus to heaven. Here we go." He opened his Bible. "From Leviticus 18:6. 'None of you may approach a woman who is closely related to uncover her nakedness.'"

"I'm glad there's a commandment in the Bible I'm happy to honor," David called out.

"I gave that up for Lent," Larry said.

"I guess I'm in trouble," Brad said. "I played doctor with my sister when we were kids."

"Did you like it?" Sam asked.

"Not much. I was the one who told on her."

"God forgives you, Brad, though your sister may still be pissed. Let's move on to scripture number two. One more from Leviticus, chapter 15, verse 16. 'When a man has a seminal discharge, any clothing or leather touched by the discharge must be washed.'"

"Monica Lewinski needs to read her Bible," Stuart said.

"Praise the Lord. I'm finally hearing the word of God," Rebecca chimed in.

"What do you mean by that?" Brian asked.

"It's rather simple, Bri. You men aren't straight shooters. You can't hit the toilet bowl either. We need to update God's laws on that one."

"At least we can aim," Brad said, chuckling.

"I'm so jealous," Rebecca said, laughing.

"Okay, here's one from Exodus. You might have to dig deep for this one. In chapter 33, Moses accuses Israel of being a stiff-necked people. What does he mean by stiff-necked?"

After some thought, Ron said, "I've got this one. He's talking about people who take Viagra by placing it under their tongue and refusing to swallow the pill."

"Nice, Ron, but again, I say enough of this shit," George said as he entered the living room carrying a bottle of wine in each hand. "I just told Alexa to play 'You Make Me Feel like a Natural Woman.'" Sam and Rebecca immediately started dancing. They were soon joined by Brian and his wife, Jane. Partygoers formed a circle around them and clapped, with some dancing on the sidelines. The Carole King song was followed by Jennifer Lopez and "I'm Real." The atmosphere was festive.

Following the Lopez song, Greg again spoke out clearly: "Alexa, stop. You guys all need to catch your breath. Here's a fourth biblical passage. This one is from Proverbs and is a little different. Tell me who this passage refers to. When he died in prison, I started believing in God again. From Proverbs 20:17. 'A man finds bread sweet when it is got by fraud, but later his mouth is full of grit.'"

"Bernie, Bernie, Bernie," Brad called out. "He made off with a lot of your money."

"That's what I hope all that jail cuisine provided him. A mouth full of grit. Okay, I've got one more, and it's easy. From Ecclesiastes 11:6. 'In the morning sow your seed, do not let your hands be idle in the evening.'"

"Queenie," George shouted out. "We can make love in the morning, and God says we can jerk off at night. You and I will reinvent the meaning of the second coming."

"I want to become a Christian," David said.

"That's music to my ears," Jesus said as he moved from the door and entered the room. "Listen, guys. I like your game, and I have a passage for you. From Luke 17:21. I can recite it for you by heart. 'The coming of the kingdom of God does not admit of observation, and there will be no one to say, look here, look there! For, you must know, the kingdom of God is among you.'"

It was as if Jesus had dropped a bomb. "I've brought you all to silence," Jesus said, laughing. "I'm not surprised. Here's what I was trying to say. The kingdom of God is not about rapture in heaven. It's about creating a community on earth where people love each other. You people here are closer to that kingdom than the congregation we met at Central Park on Monday evening. But enough of this. I need some wine. As you will learn from reading the gospel of Luke, I love to party."

The party continued in the same exuberant spirit until well after one in the morning. Jesus made the rounds, introducing himself to all of the guests, all smiles and full of pleasant small talk. At one point, sometime after ten, Jesus cornered Jonathan and asked him if they could go to a private place for an extended chat. Jonathan led him to the den.

"Okay, my new friend," Jesus said as he sat down on the love seat. "You are my top candidate for becoming my messenger. You are a gifted musician, which will add to your appeal, and your sexual orientation makes you a symbol of inclusion, which is one of my more important values that needs to be communicated."

"Wow, I'm speechless," Jonathan replied, smiling across at Jesus. "I assume this position will require a lot of public speaking. I have done very little of that in my career."

"It's a learned skill," Jesus said. "Because you're so good in front of people with your guitar, I'm sure you will learn quickly."

"But I know so little about the New Testament."

"That I can teach you. I have summarized the message I want you to communicate in this little blue book." Jesus handed it to him. "It's not very complicated. Can we spend maybe half an hour together so I can give you some idea of what you'd be speaking about?"

"Absolutely. I'm already at home. I'm going nowhere."

"Here's one of the big problems that needs to be dealt with. People have no idea who I was as a first-century man. It may surprise you to learn I was married and that I lost my beautiful wife in childbirth. That was a common scourge when we were having children."

"That is surprising. Why has it been kept a secret for all these years?"

"Because Nazareth was such a tiny village—maybe three hundred residents when I lived there. No one had an interest in writing about a Galilean peasant from our little village.

"This problem was compounded by the Roman destruction of Jerusalem in 70 CE. The movement in my name under my brother James was wiped out. Few survived. People who knew anything about my youth were among those who lost their lives. Judaism in Jerusalem was also destroyed. Our movement at that time was a Jewish sect. We coexisted with other Jews within the synagogue.

"Jews who survived the Roman invasion—and there weren't many—fled to cities in the Hellenistic world. The Gospels were written in those cities many years later by people who knew nothing about the first thirty years of my life. So they made up stories about me like the silly idea that God was my father and my mother was a virgin. Believe me, Joseph was my father, and my parents had an active sex life that produced five children.

"Here's the problem with all of this. Because history knows so little about my life in rural Galilee, Christians are able to invent their own Jesus. That's how I became known as the Son of God and was made into the second arm of the Trinity. Like the virgin-birth myth, these are silly ideas that have no anchor in reality."

"I can see how that can be a problem."

"I want people to know the real Jesus, not some mythological figure they have invented. I want people to know what I was all about in the first century. Again, my message was simple. I wanted my people to know in a deep sense the God of love that so graced my life. Religion is not about what you believe but rather about a heart that overflows with love. People with a loving heart are inclusive, they work to remediate the problems of economic and social injustice, and they seek nonviolent solutions to problems.

"I want you to deliver that simple message. Our current world is in a bad way. There is the climate crisis, several countries possess weapons of mass destruction, world military spending is out of control, economic distribution in your country has never been so skewed in favor of the rich, and then there is this COVID crisis. I believe my teachings are as relevant today as they were two thousand years ago. I'm looking for someone to make that point."

"I do have a real sense of a loving God in my life, but there are so many points of church doctrine that make little sense to me. I grew up in the Episcopal Church and left because I could not recite the creeds with a straight face."

"Have you not been listening to me?" Jesus asked with a laugh as he left the love seat to embrace Jonathan. "You are perfect for the job. The point is to be rid of all the foolish doctrine and focus on learning how to love," Jesus said as he hugged Jonathan one more time before returning to his seat.

"Okay, I do get it," Jonathan said, smiling over at Jesus. "I'm not sure I'm the right guy to become your messenger, but I certainly will consider it. Before we go back to the party, I do have one more question. If the New Testament has so many problems, how could you come back?"

Jesus laughed, looked at Jonathan, and said, "That's a really good question. Let me answer it this way. The end of life is a deep mystery. What happens after we die is the last question for which we will receive an answer. In the meantime, here is my passionate plea. Let's worry about now. Let's work together to create a society and a world that is sustainable and one in which every human being has a real opportunity to achieve his or her true potential."

"That's a wonderful vision, Jesus. You are getting to me. Let me sleep on this messenger thing, and we can talk about it in the morning. Please spend the night with us, and I promise to give you an answer in the morning. In the meantime, I need to get back to the party. My buddies love to sing."

❧

The three slept late on Sunday morning after finally getting to bed at 2 a.m. following the cleanup. Jonathan had made his decision the night before, but he wanted to discuss it with George first before giving Jesus a definite answer. "Queenie, I agree with Jesus. You would be perfect for the job. You would also do a lot of good for the gay rights movement. I don't give a rat's ass about religion, but there is something about you, Jesus, that tells me you're the real deal. I say do it, Queenie."

Jonathan jumped up from his seat at the breakfast table to hug his partner. "This makes it so much easier. You're the best, my love."

"I've got an idea for you guys. Rosie McDonald was my patient. I think I could get you both on her show. You could make the big announcement there before a national TV audience."

"You are the best, George. That would really jump-start our efforts," Jesus said with a warm smile.

4

The Scene

JESUS MOVED IN WITH George and Jonathan following the party, which eased his financial concerns to a large degree. He spent considerable time with Jonathan, educating him on New Testament issues and reassuring him that he was the man for the job. With Jonathan's help, he learned how to use the internet and was able to find the website for Stillwater Baptist Church. Wednesday night at 7:30 was Bible study at the church, and he decided to attend.

He arrived at the church at 7:40 p.m. and was led by a custodian to the basement, where he found Dr. Norcross leading a class of about twenty members. As he stood at the doorway of the classroom, a female member of the group asked Dr. Norcross, "How long must we wait for the rapture? I have Jeremy's college-tuition bill on my desk. Should I pay it?"

"Pay it by all means, Victoria," Dr. Norcross replied. "Money will have no meaning when our Jesus returns. The Bible promises it will be imminent. Let us review this evening the prophet Daniel's famous vision of the coming of the son of man. That explains it all. Please turn to chapter 7 of Daniel in your Bibles."

"Hi, I'm back," Jesus said as he entered the room. "Sorry to be late for your class. Do you mind if I take a seat? If you're examining Daniel, you must still have the rapture on your mind."

"Class, let me introduce Jesus, the imposter," Dr. Norcross said. "We welcome all committed Christians to our table. You may remove your mask, Mr. Imposter. You are among true believers who place their protection in the hands of God."

"Thank you, Julian. Can I make a brief comment about the book of Daniel?"

"Please do. We are open to all opinions at Stillwater Baptist."

"The book is a work of fraud."

"That's a rather arrogant charge from someone who obviously knows nothing about our sacred Scriptures," Dr. Norcross responded in a voice of some passion.

"The writer in the first chapter claims to live in the sixth century BCE, but he was, in fact, born four hundred years later."

"What do you mean by BCE?" a male class member asked.

"The initials stand for 'before the Common Era.' We used to say 'BC' to make this point. You know, before me. Now, here's the problem with Daniel. The writer makes many statements that appear to be prophetic. He wants you to think the book was written in the sixth century before me, that he is predicting the future when he writes about certain events; but he is actually writing history, about events that had already taken place. The book was actually written in the second century BCE, 167 years before I was born. His strategy is to impress his listeners—most sacred scripture was listened to rather than read in those days—with his prophetic ability. As a result, listeners would be in awe of his prediction of the coming son of man. The author deliberately misleads his listeners. He claims to be someone he is not, with the result that the work should be stricken from the canon."

"Your charges are obviously false, totally without support," Dr. Norcross responded. "Please return to wearing your mask. We don't want to hear anything further from you."

"What are you suggesting?" a male class member asked. "That our Jesus in the person of the Son of Man will not return? That the rapture may not take place?"

"That's exactly what I'm suggesting. Julian said in response to one of your earlier questions that the rapture is imminent. People have been saying that for two thousand years."

"Why do so many Christians believe it, then?" a female member of the class asked Jesus.

"Muslims have similar beliefs, but that doesn't make them true," Jesus responded.

"Muslims believe in the rapture?" a male class member asked.

"There are interesting parallels between Christian and Shia Muslim beliefs about the end of time."

"Is that what all that virgin stuff is about?" the man continued. "Those crazy terrorists believed they would be rewarded in heaven for their crimes."

"They must be terribly disappointed up there," Jesus responded with a smile.

"What do you mean, 'up there'?" Dr. Norcross called out. "What are they doing in our heaven, Jesus, or whoever you are?"

"I guess you could say they are looking for love in all the wrong places," Jesus said with a chuckle.

"Looking for love?" Dr. Norcross continued.

"If they are still looking for all those virgins, I would imagine they're pretty horny by now," Jesus said with a smile.

"Horny?" Dr. Norcross called out.

"Yes. Being horny is a physical condition that results from the absence of one's lover," Jesus responded.

"I know what horny means," Dr. Norcross screamed out.

"That's good, sir. I hope it's not a condition you experience often."

"This is an outrage," Dr. Norcross called out with vehemence. "Get out of here, you evil imposter, and we ask that you never bring your blasphemy to our church again." Jesus left the church, convinced these people would believe all the nonsense regarding the rapture to their graves.

❧

Jonathan and Jesus were scheduled to appear on *The Scene*, Rosie McDonald's popular afternoon talk show, on Tuesday, the day after Labor Day. In preparation, Jonathan went on Friday morning to have his hair cut by his friend Daniel.

"Danny, my man, I'm here for a new look," Jonathan said, smiling at his friend, who was sweeping his shop free of hair.

Daniel, dressed in a muscle shirt, jeans rolled up to his knees, white tennis shoes, pearls, and a pink beret in his hair, spoke with a dramatic hand motion: "My chair is yours." Daniel placed a protective smock on Jonathan, carefully smoothed it out, touched Jonathan's face lovingly, and stroked his hair. "You're pressuring me, my dear, dear friend. Only twenty-five minutes to achieve your new look. It can't be done." In preparation, he began by arranging Jonathan's hair with several bobby pins. "I'm an artist, my Queenie. It's inconsiderate of you, this time constraint."

"Sorry about that, Danny. My schedule is really crowded today."

"I hear your friend Jesus was at your party last week," Daniel said while circling the chair and singing out, "I'm a believer. I'm a believer. He's my guy."

"He's the best, Danny. I can assure you of that."

"I'm a celebrity stylist. I'm a celebrity stylist," Daniel sang out while continuing to dance around the chair.

"What's this all about?" Jonathan asked with a broad smile.

"Can I be the first to kiss the new Messiah on the cheek?" He ended his dance to give Jonathan a big kiss on the lips.

"I guess news travels fast," Jonathan said while looking in the mirror. "Danny, what are you doing with my hair? This is not about some drag-queen beauty contest. I need to look straight for this new gig."

"You mean I can't do your nails?"

"There's no time for that, Danny."

"Oh my, Queenie, Queenie, Queenie. You're acting like a celebrity. There's no time but your time."

"Just a heavy trim," Jonathan said while again smiling at his friend. "I'll be more cooperative next time I'm here."

"You're much too beautiful for the straight look, my dear, dear Messiah."

"George likes me best that way."

"He has no taste, my Queenie. You know that. You're an artist, a celebrity. Let me loan you my earrings, some pearls."

"I need a more simple look when speaking for Jesus."

"He's not sending you to the Amish, my Queenie. You're speaking to the world, for all of us. You're speaking for God."

"How does one speak for God, Danny?"

"In a high voice, my Queenie."

"Does God really communicate with human beings?"

"God speaks to me. The other day, I heard God's voice: 'Daniel, namesake of my favorite prophet, your nails are stunning in bright pink.' And Queenie, you will never doubt God's word when you hear this. God told me to date Kevin." Daniel danced around his chair. "'How can I not like an Irishman, my Daniel?' is what God said."

"Next time you speak with him . . ."

"Oh, God is a she, my Queenie. I'm glad we had this conversation. You can't be speaking for Jesus and be confused about gender."

"There's so much I have to learn, Danny. Tell me why you think God is female."

"I know so, my Queenie. Would a male God be complimenting me on my nails?"

"I see your point."

"We talk recipes too. She loves my crêpe suzette."

"What did she tell you to do with your Tampax?"

"She told me to keep some on hand. You never know."

"That's what I love best about God. It's all a mystery."

"Not to me, my Queenie. I know you are the new Messiah, and my God loves me in pearls," Daniel said as he began removing the smock from Jonathan.

"Thanks for the great haircut and all of the good advice. I'll see you in a few weeks."

"Hit a home run on Rosie, my Queenie. I'll be watching. We're all so proud of you."

Jonathan and Jesus arrived at the studio for the Rosie McDonald show at 1:45 in the afternoon on September 7th. They were taken to the office of Sandra Halligan, the show's producer, who led them to a small dressing room directly adjacent to the set. They were told they were Rosie's first guests and that a stagehand would take them to their places at 2:55.

"Thank you. Thank you very much. The three ladies beside me need no introduction—Barbie Waters, Betsy Hazelbach, and Joyce Balfor. I'm Rosie McDonald." The audience broke out in applause. "Thank you again. Thank you so much. I want to start our show this morning by paying tribute to my mom. She is an active ninety-year-old who lives in Daytona Beach, Florida. She was out riding her bike two weeks ago and came home winded. It scared her; she worried about her heart, so she went to see her primary care physician. After receiving a series of tests, she was pronounced 100 percent fit. Naturally, she was thrilled to be on her bike again. As she started to climb the short hill outside her apartment building, feeling a little winded for a second time, she began to worry. As she crested the hill, the old maintenance man yelled out to her, 'Hey, Mrs. McDonald. Your back tire is flat.'

"To be fair, I have to tell one on my dad. He died five years ago; and sadly, toward the end, he was a little confused. One day around noon, he went into the public library, and in a loud voice ordered a cheeseburger, fries, and a small coke. 'This is a library, sir,' the lady behind the desk said. My dad responded in a very quiet voice: 'I'll have a cheeseburger, fries, and a small coke.'

"When I saw all the Christians waiting for Jesus, I called my friend Tom to see if any of his Scientology buddies were among them. He told me that humans work out their salvation on earth, that we are immortal spiritual beings who have forgotten our true nature. Let me show you all my ring finger." She paused to raise her left hand. "I'm going to change fingers. I certainly don't want to forget who I really am.

"You all will be proud of me. I've gone green. I recently purchased a new smart car. You know, one of those tiny little things that gets amazing gas mileage. The carbon admissions are said to be lower, lots lower. The only problem I haven't solved is getting into the car. But not to worry. I'm thinking of a diet. It's a real dilemma. On the one hand, the more weight I lose, the easier it will be to kidnap me. On the other hand, I need to get into that damn car. You figure!

"We've got a great show for today, though I admit it's a little different. Our first guest you won't recognize, but I'm sure you have all heard of him. So don't leave your seat. We'll be right back."

As the commercial break concluded, Rosie continued: "Our first guest needs no introduction. You have all read about him, prayed to him, and sang about him. Will you please welcome Jesus of Nazareth." There was a gasp in the audience as Jesus entered the set. He shook hands with the four women, sat down in the vacant chair, and smiled at the audience. "You know, Jesus. We have a big problem here. Nobody is going to believe it is you."

"Make a little wine for us, Jesus. It's five in the afternoon somewhere," Joyce said, laughing.

"That's getting a little trite, Joyce," Jesus responded with a smile. "How about a prediction? You know, the kind of thing the prophets were famous for doing. I predict those expecting the imminent coming of the rapture will have to wait another two thousand years."

"That's sad news for our fundamentalist friends," Betsy said.

"I can't wait to hear their excuses as they continue to wait," Rosie said.

"They're good at changing the goalposts," Jesus interjected.

"So is my good friend Mr. Frump," Rosie said while smiling at Jesus. "We got through August without his retaking the White House. I wonder what date his insurrectionist friends will set next?"

"The more relevant date is when he will go to jail," Joyce said.

"Girls, girls, girls. It's best we love our enemies," Jesus said while laughing.

"I'll love him best from jail," Joyce said.

"He's got all that orange hair slicked up with bottles of spray. It's hard to love a punk rocker, but let's change the subject," Rosie said. "What I want to know is this. If this isn't the rapture, why have you come back?"

"That's an important question. Thank you for asking it. I came back to remind people to love their neighbor, to live the love you sense in your heart, to help the poor and the less privileged, to be inclusive, to give peace a chance. That's how you find God in your life, not by believing in me as one cool dude."

"I really do think of you as one cool dude," Betsy said.

"Well, thank you, Betsy. That's really nice."

"I have a question for you," Joyce said. "I'm dying to know if Mary was a perpetual virgin or if she and Joseph really did it."

"La, la, la, la, la," Jesus said, covering his ears and laughing. "Children, you know, have a hard time thinking about the sex lives of their parents. However, if I have to answer your question, let me say I hope my mother wasn't a perpetual virgin. She would have missed out on a lot of fun. Making love together is one of God's greatest gifts to us."

"How did I miss that lesson in Sunday school?" Rosie asked.

"Probably because your teachers were not as good as my new messenger."

"Nice lead-in, kid," Rosie said, smiling across at Jesus. "It is indeed a good time to introduce your new messenger. Would you please welcome Mr. Jonathan Thurman." Jonathan walked onto the stage, shook hands with the four women, smiled at Jesus, and took a seat. The audience offered polite applause, after which Rosie continued. "Well, Jonathan. I guess it's safe to say your life has changed in the last few days."

"That would be an understatement."

"Tell us how you are doing with it," Rosie said.

"It's really exciting and, I must admit, a little scary."

"I imagine so," Betsy interjected. "Have you ever done anything like this before?"

"The simple answer is no."

"Jonathan's the best, folks," Jesus said, smiling at his friend. "I can guarantee that. Wait till you hear him sing."

"We definitely want to do that," Rosie said, "but before we do, I would like to know a little about your plans. What will you be doing as Jesus' messenger?"

"Well, next month I'll be in Colorado. My partner, Dr. George Saunders, has a medical meeting at the Keystone Lodge. Jesus wants me to deliver a formal apology on his behalf to the medical profession at that meeting."

"Dr. Saunders is the best, folks. He took care of my gallstone problem four years ago," Rosie said.

"That sounds intriguing," Betsy said. "Can you give us any hints of what you plan to say?"

Jonathan looked over at Jesus, who gestured no. "No, Betsy. I'm honor bound to let the doctors know first."

"You and Jesus are learning how to play the media game real well," Rosie said. "Keep us guessing. Your announcement should attract quite an audience."

"I hope so," Jesus said.

"Your remarks should be interesting," Betsy said. "I don't often think of Jesus making mistakes."

"I hope I didn't make many, Betsy, but this is a big one that needs correcting."

"Well, we all want to hear Jonathan sing. Get your guitar, and while you're doing that, we'll take a question from the audience."

"Who will be our first woman president?" a woman from the audience yelled out.

"Hillary Clinton came close, but I think we should draft Rosie for 2024." The audience erupted in loud cheers.

"I'll do it if you'll be my running mate."

"I'm not eligible. I wasn't born in the USA."

Rosie and Jonathan, who had returned with his guitar, broke out mimicking Springsteen's famous chorus: "Born in the USA. He wasn't born in the USA."

"Hey, Jesus," Rosie said while laughing. "We could say you were born again in the USA. That would help us get the evangelical vote."

"You'd have to get yourself a new partner," Joyce interjected.

"I'm afraid you're right. We'll have to save this for another time. I see you're ready, Jonathan. What do you have for us?"

"This is a new song I have written for a tour I hope to make in the fall to begin spreading Jesus' message. Jesus taught me that the first principle of living a spiritual life is to 'simply be.'" Jonathan began with an artful guitar introduction and then began singing:

I'm in this moment now, and this is all I have.
I choose to be here now, and this is who I am.

I've come to find this peace of mind.
I'm more aware all the time.

I can see myself each day living in the flow.
Accepting life the way it is, just by letting go.

I will listen to my heart, allowing it to lead
And I've discovered it's enough just to simply be.

I owe it to the world to live my life this way.
I know that peace will come, and love will lead the way.

I have come to find this quiet mind.
I'm more aware all of the time.

I can see myself each day living in the flow
Accepting life the way it is just by letting go.

I believe that life will give everything I need.
And I require nothing more than to simply be.

5

Jesus on Trial

TWO WEEKS AFTER THEIR appearance on *The Scene*, some amazing things had happened. The phone was ringing off the hook. They already had a list of 1,479 people who were interested in helping create a movement. Jonathan had trained Jesus on how to enter their names in a database. They also had a little more than $32,000 in the bank.

Jonathan was eager to build on that momentum. He summarized many of the points in Jesus' little blue book and took it to the local print shop to have 250 brochures made. Jonathan picked up the brochures on Monday, September 20th, and on Tuesday, he and Jesus made the half-hour walk to Grand Central Station to hand them out.

Located at the junction of Forty-Second Street and Park Avenue in Midtown Manhattan, Grand Central Station is the third-largest train station in North America. It is one of the most popular tourist attractions in New York City because of the beautiful Beaux-Arts architecture of the buildings. Beaux-Arts is a French architectural style that combines elements of both Gothic and Renaissance design. It was one of Jonathan's favorite land-marks in the city.

Standing outside the façade of the central building, Jonathan walked toward the first traveler to pass by. "Hi, my name is Jonathan. I'd like to introduce you to my friend Jesus. Here is our brochure." He handed it to the man. "At some point during the day, you might take a look at it."

"Thanks, man. I love Jesus. Look forward to it." The man tossed the brochure into the trash receptacle not twenty yards from where they were standing.

A middle-aged woman passed them next, and Jonathan made a similar introduction. The woman refused the brochure and shouted out, "Go back to Israel, buddy. They welcome illegal immigrants there."

They had a little more luck with the next man to emerge from the building. "You're just the guy I'm looking for," he said.

"That's nice," Jesus responded. "What can I do for you?"

The man took his hat off and said, "As you can see, I'm bald, and all I can tell you is that you don't listen very well at night."

"I take it you're praying for more hair," Jesus said with a smile.

As he was speaking, Jonathan gently poked him and whispered, "We have company. Dr. Norcross has assembled a group of about twenty-five people who have gathered across the street at Thomas Paine Park to protest us."

"That should make things interesting," Jesus whispered back before directing his attention to the man with no hair.

"How did you guess?" the man said.

"Have you heard about the Muslims making a pilgrimage to Mecca to make special prayer requests?"

"I knew they went there," the man responded, "but I didn't know why."

"Well, in a similar spirit, make a pilgrimage to a little place in North Carolina called Morehead City, and pray to me from there. I think that would help to get my attention." Jesus paused, laughing at his attempt at humor, and said, "I'm just pulling your leg. I mean no harm."

"Fuck you, man, and here's your damn brochure."

"I get the hair request often," Jesus said to Jonathan.

"Next time he prays, send him a comb," Jonathan said with a smile. "The Norcross group is starting to make some noise. Isn't this fun!"

"Send the imposter back to Israel." A man shouted out from the crowd.

"Send that little pervert with him," another protestor screamed out. Undeterred, Jonathan gave his introduction and handed the brochure to an older woman who approached them with a smile.

"Thanks," the woman responded. "I need something to read this morning."

The menacing attacks from the Norcross protestors persisted as an older man with a cane slowly approached and was handed a brochure. "Is this the second coming or some Mormon scheme? Am I going to burn?"

"No one will burn," Jesus responded. "I'm here to say there won't be a second coming. It was all a big mistake."

"So now you're telling me the Bible's a scam. What's a poor old guy like me to believe?"

"Maybe our brochure can help in that regard," Jonathan said, smiling across at the man.

"I'll look it over, but don't ask me to give up my internet porn. It's all an old guy like me has left."

A young man entered the scene, refused the brochure, and gave them the finger as he passed by. "I love you too," the young man said with a smirk on his face.

"Why is that guy waving his middle finger at us?" Jesus asked.

"He's saying hi to the pigeons over there." Jonathan pointed to three pigeons scouring the street for scraps to eat. "It's his way of blessing them."

"He seemed a little angry to me."

"It's called 'giving them the bird.' It's a well-known way for Americans to express blessing."

Jesus liked that explanation, and an idea popped into his head. He crossed the street, walking to Thomas Paine Park and waving his middle finger to bless the Norcross protestors. What happened next stunned Jesus. The protestors lunged at him. As Jonathan ran across the street in an attempt to stop Jesus, they punched him hard in the stomach. Jesus was pushed, shoved, and screamed at. When the police came to investigate, Jesus, in desperation, gave them the finger too and was promptly arrested. Jonathan returned to 400 Riverside Drive in a panic.

Jesus was taken to the Brooklyn Detention Center on Atlantic Avenue and placed in a single cell. The complex was used primarily as a place to house detainees awaiting trial. The supporters of Jesus received some good news with regard to the trial. Jonathan and George had a lawyer friend who was well connected with the New York judicial system. While Hank Pierson could not get Jesus out of jail, he was able to get a speedy trial. The trial was set for nine in the morning on Friday, September 24th, at the County Courthouse at Foley Square. The presiding judge, Laura O'Brien, was interested in the case because of what she had heard about the appearance of Jonathan and Jesus on *The Scene*. She rearranged her schedule accordingly.

At eight thirty on the day of the trial, the Reverend Dr. Julian Norcross assembled another group of protestors, who gathered at the entrance to the courthouse. "My fellow Christians. Today the imposter will be brought to justice," Dr. Norcross called out.

"Crucify him. Crucify the bloody bastard," came from the crowd.

"Let no one be fooled. Satan is our enemy. We will fight him in the guise of this imposter."

"And that pervert he hangs around with," again came from the crowd.

"We will fight him in the guise of the liberal news establishment," Dr. Norcross fumed.

"Fox News forever," came from the crowd.

"We will fight him in the guise of the global-warming hoax," Norcross shouted.

"Bless the soul of Rush Limbaugh for exposing all those greenie perverts," came from the crowd.

"We will fight him in the guise of the sinister gun-control lobby," Norcross called out.

From the crowd: "Charlton Heston, you're our man."

"We will fight him in the guise of radical feminism."

"Sarah Palin, we love you."

"My fellow Christians. Our Jesus will return from the clouds of heaven. This imposter flew in a plane."

"Send him back, send him back," the crowd screamed out. One fellow added, "To the Jew-land where he belongs."

"God is our Father," Dr. Norcross intoned. "Christ is our Savior. You all out there are his army." Cheers erupted from the crowd. "God blesses you. God thanks you for being here today. Your heavenly Father will reward you in heaven."

"And he will send that pervert messenger to hell," a man from the crowd yelled out. And then, all of a sudden, there was silence as two police cars approached and parked in front of the courthouse. Jesus emerged from the back seat of the lead car in handcuffs. As he proceeded through the crowd, he was jeered at and spit upon, and a few tried to punch him. His two police escorts rushed to get him out of harm's way.

"All rise," the bailiff called out. "Case of Jesus Christ verses the City of New York, Judge Laura O'Brien presiding."

Judge Laura entered the courtroom from a door behind her bench, took her seat, and surveyed the courtroom. "Will the defendant please stand. I understand, Mr. Christ, you have decided to represent yourself. Is that correct?"

"Yes, it is, your honor. I have a little experience in this regard. The last time I appeared in court I was convicted by the crowd. If the crowd maintains their silence, I think I have a good chance of being acquitted."

"No one will speak in this courtroom without being duly recognized. It might provide greater clarity with regard to your testimony, Jesus, if you removed your mask. Have you been fully vaccinated?"

"Yes, your honor. I do have one additional favor to ask. Can you release me from these handcuffs? They have become terribly uncomfortable."

"I think we can do that, Mr. Christ. Bailiff, will you please take the cuffs off for the defendant."

"Big mistake, your honor," a man from the audience yelled out. "This Satanic fraud is a dangerous threat to our society."

"This is my first and my last warning. The next person to speak out without being recognized will be taken from the court." Turning to Jesus, she said, "Is that better, Mr. Christ?"

"Much better, your honor. Thank you very much."

"Okay, Mr. Christ. It is time for you to come forward so we can swear you in." There was a brief pause as Jesus approached the bench. "Place your right hand on the Bible for me, please."

"My favorite book, your honor," Jesus said, smiling up at the judge.

"Do you swear to tell the truth, the whole truth, so help you God?"

"I do."

"Please state your name for the court."

"Jesus."

"And your last name, please."

"There is no last name, your honor. Christ was added by the church. Those early church fathers took lots of liberties. They made me into something I am not. It would be nice to sue them on several counts, but I suppose we have a statute-of-limitations problem."

"I suspect we would. Where did you say you lived?"

"In Nazareth. There were no streets in the first century. Only narrow footpaths. So just put down Nazareth. It was a tiny place. We knew all the neighbors."

"Sounds nice, Jesus. And now, how do you plead to the charges of disorderly conduct and assaulting a police officer?"

"I am innocent of all charges, your honor."

"Liar. The man's a dirty liar. Crucify the son of a bitch."

Judge Laura looked to her left at a policeman. "Remove the man in the Yankees cap with the Obama-to-Kenya T-shirt from the courtroom, please." There was a pause in the proceedings as this order was carried out. "Now, Jesus, back to the charges, which state that on September 21th you were inciting a riot by giving a group of protestors the finger and you also assaulted a police officer."

"I was merely blessing them, your honor. I didn't realize it took two fingers raised in a V shape to make a peace sign."

"I can explain all this, your honor," Jonathan said as he stepped forward. "I don't mean to be speaking out of turn, but the whole matter was a misunderstanding for which I am responsible."

"And you are?"

"Jonathan Thurman, Jesus' messenger, your honor."

"Pervert, pervert. Dirty homo pervert."

"Who made that toxic utterance?" And the judge paused. There was silence in the courtroom. Eventually, Judge Laura continued. "Unless someone owns up to it, I'm going to slap a $5,000 fine on your church. I thought I made myself clear about speaking without recognition."

"Dom, stand up, please," Dr. Norcross said in a voice close to a whisper. "The church can't afford such a fine. God will reward you in heaven for your forthright statement." A short man in a blue T-shirt with tattoos on both arms slowly rose from his seat in the audience.

"Remove him, Harold," the judge said, looking to her left at the police officer again. "Let me add this warning: the $5,000 fine will be levied if any further outbursts occur." When Harold returned to his place to the left of the bench, Judge Laura continued. "Okay, Mr. Thurman. Would you please step forward so I can swear you in. Jesus, you remain next to Mr. Thurman in case I have additional questions for you." The judge moved the Bible toward Jonathan. "Place your right hand on the Bible, please. Do you swear to tell the truth, the whole truth, so help you God?"

"I do."

"State your name and address for the court."

"Jonathan Thurman, 400 Riverside Drive, New York City."

"Thank you, Mr. Thurman. Now your explanation, please."

"I appreciate this opportunity, your honor. It's a long story."

"Give us every delicious detail," Mr. Thurman. "I'm warming up to this trial."

"Jesus and I were handing out brochures at Grand Central on the morning of September 21st. When Jesus offered this man a brochure, he refused the brochure and gave Jesus the finger instead. Because Jesus was not familiar with some of the less-than-friendly gestures in our society, he was confused about the man's actions. I created the misunderstanding by telling Jesus the man was blessing him, that the middle finger was a sign of blessing. Jesus' instinct is to bless his enemies, so he went into the crowd of protestors, giving them the finger. A fight ensued. When the police came to break up the fight, Jesus blessed a policeman with the finger. He wasn't assaulting the officer, your honor, just blessing him."

"Is this an accurate description of these events, Jesus?"

"Yes, it is, your honor."

"Are there members of that protest group here in the courtroom gallery?"

"Yes, your honor," Jesus responded. "I noticed their leader, Dr. Julian Norcross, when I was being led into the courtroom."

Judge Laura looked out at the spectators. "Dr. Norcross, will you please approach the bench." She paused as Dr. Norcross made his way through the courtroom to the judge's bench. "Dr. Norcross, you have heard the testimony of Jesus of Nazareth regarding the incident at Grand Central Station. He testified that he thought he was blessing you. Are you willing to forgive Jesus for a gesture he made that day that he didn't fully understand?"

"No, your honor. Only God Almighty can forgive."

"I'm not surprised, Dr. Norcross. You may be seated. Jesus, please give Dr. Norcross your one-fingered salute as he makes his way back to his seat. This case is dismissed. The defendant is innocent of all charges."

6

An Unusual Apology

THE OPENING SESSION FOR George's medical convention at the convention hall at Keystone, Colorado, took place at 9:00 a.m. on October 8th. After welcoming all the doctors to Colorado, Dr. James Gardner introduced George. George entered the hall, surveyed the audience, shook hands warmly with Dr. Gardner, and slowly proceeded to the lectern.

"Thank you, Dr. Gardner, for that kind introduction. As all of you are aware, September was an eventful month. Many of you may have seen on television or heard about the appearance of Jonathan Thurman on *The Scene* with Jesus four weeks ago. At one of their earlier meetings together, Jesus asked Jonathan, my partner for the last twenty years, to issue a formal apology on his behalf to the medical profession at this meeting. Because of the unusual circumstances surrounding this request, our meeting organizers have graciously consented to give Jonathan ten minutes to deliver this apology from Jesus. With that said, would you please welcome Mr. Jonathan Thurman to the podium. Jonathan, old buddy, we look forward to your remarks with great interest." George left the podium, hugged Jonathan as he entered, and stepped off stage.

Jonathan also began by surveying the audience, and before speaking, he broke into a broad smile. "Thank you, George, and I also want to thank the organizing committee for allowing me to deliver this unusual message on such short notice. I consented to be Jesus' messenger with deep misgivings, fearing that serving in such a role would only lead to ridicule. This is my first public appearance on his behalf, and I must admit to being a little nervous. In addition, as you will soon see, I have little experience as a public speaker, and I'm certainly not well schooled on theological issues. I also know that these confessions of humility are beginning to sound like the disclaimers that follow a drug commercial, so I better get on with it.

"As George mentioned, Jesus wants to issue a formal apology to the medical profession. Here is his concern. He believes many doctors have had problems with the New Testament and with their faith generally because of the miracle stories. The healing miracles do not make sense to trained medical professionals. The problem you will be interested to learn is not with doctors but with the New Testament.

"People knew nothing about the biological causes of disease in the first century, Jesus told me. Disease was believed to be caused instead by Satan, by evil forces invading the body. Healing was a matter of getting right with God, of ending the control of Satan over one's body. When Jesus is pictured curing disease in the New Testament, his cures are always associated with defeating the forces of evil, with defeating Satan. Jesus did not cure disease the way you do.

"The Gospel writers report the deeds of Jesus through the lens of a first-century worldview. This worldview is often at odds with twenty-first-century thinking. Jesus now has a far better understanding of disease than he had two thousand years ago. If the healing-miracle stories in the New Testament have been a stumbling block for your faith, Jesus apologizes. Again, it's the problem of the New Testament, not your problem.

"That's it. Are there any questions?"

A man from the audience called out: "Can you give us an example?"

"Sure. Read the miracle stories in the Gospel of Luke with a focus on chapters 4 to 9. In each case when Jesus heals, he is battling Satan, not dealing with the biological causes of the disease like you do. The other Gospels agree with Luke on this question, but reading Luke should be enough to convince you. It won't take but half an hour."

Another person from the audience called out: "Why do you believe in this guy? This whole thing is incredible to me."

"Because he is willing to admit a mistake. That doesn't happen often in our society." Jonathan paused briefly to let that sink in before continuing. "But that's just the tip of the iceberg.

"I am gay. What does society say about me, a gay man? 'He is queer.' The nasty ones say, 'His lifestyle is disgusting.' Many people only see me through the lens of my sexual orientation. What do Christians say about me? Many claim my sexual orientation is a sin.

"What does Jesus say, in contrast? I love you unconditionally. Your sexual orientation makes no difference to me. Jesus sees me as a whole person. When I am with him, the love in my heart overflows. It has changed me. That's why I'm here. That's why I believe in him."

As George slowly walked toward the lectern, Jonathan turned and smiled at him. "George is my cue that my time is up. Thank you so much for your polite attention. George has meetings until 3:00 p.m. While he is occupied, I plan to take my guitar to a secluded area on the south side of this hall. If any of you have questions or would just like to talk, please join me. I look forward to meeting real flesh-and-blood healers of the twenty-first century."

Half an hour later, a woman approached the bench where Jonathan was sitting with his guitar. "Hi, I'm Ellen."

Jonathan got up from the bench to shake her hand and said, "Jonathan, nice to meet you."

"I really liked your answer about why you believe in Jesus."

"Thanks. Come sit. You must be a doc."

"I practice part-time in the Pittsburgh area."

"Part-time?"

"Well, we have two kids. Two energetic little boys. My husband teaches biology and coaches at the high school."

"How does a part-time doctor fit into a medical practice?"

"I take call two nights a week, see patients at a clinic on Thursdays, and operate on Fridays. I gathered from your little talk this morning that Jesus inspires you."

"That's it exactly. I am inspired by the beauty of his character, by the peacefulness of his being. He lives love. I want to be that way too. The miraculous stuff doesn't interest me much."

"What about the salvation stuff?"

"As Jesus said to me one night at a party, what happens at the end of life is a mystery. I consented to do this work because I'm concerned with life now. The central theme of this little handbook by Jesus," and he paused to hand her a copy, "is that humans have a second chance. We can make our culture and society more loving, less materialistic, more peaceful. We can make the world a better place to live."

"How? I mean, it all sounds so nice."

"It's up to you, Ellen. You change. You develop habits of caring. You care for your children in a way that enables them to be psychologically healthy. You conduct your work in a way that combines healing and compassion. You use your resources to help others. Do you see what I mean? I'm not picking on you."

"Absolutely. It's a beautiful vision. How doctrinaire is he?"

"That's the main point of his message. Religion is not about doctrine or belief. Religious doctrine is a human creation and has nothing to do with relating to God. We're talking about the virgin birth, the physical resurrection, the atoning sacrifice on the cross—all that stuff. True religion is about a full heart, a heart overflowing with love.

"He gave me this wonderful example of the church councils in the fifth century. There was confusion among Christians surrounding the nature of Jesus, it was causing real conflict, and political leaders wanted the conflict to end. As a result, they called on bishops to get together in councils to work out their differences.

"You would think that if the doctrine that came out of these councils was true, that if it really reflected the word of God, bishops would have sat together in circles, holding hands with their eyes closed, waiting for God to speak to them. Unfortunately, that's not at all what happened.

"In 449, at the Second Council of Ephesus, a slight majority of bishops believed Jesus was fully divine, a God walking the earth. To win the day, dissenting bishops were beat up by armed thugs. Those on the fence were bribed and threatened. Council participants engaged in name calling, slander, and intimidation.

"Soon after the council had arrived at this conclusion, an amazing thing happened. The king who organized the council—and I wish I could remember his name—anyway, this guy who had been a firm believer in the full divinity of Jesus fell off a horse and died. This allowed those favoring a more balanced Jesus, one fully human and fully divine, whatever that means, to regroup and call for a new council.

"The bishops met at Chalcedon in 451. Through a similar process of bribery and intimidation, creeds were agreed upon and Jesus became fully human/fully divine. The Trinity was enshrined. Had that king not fallen from his horse, there would have been no Chalcedon. Jesus would have been forever viewed as fully divine, as God wandering the earth.

"Sadly, however, this did not end the dispute. The two sides fought for the next two hundred years. Because state power was weak during those days and unable to control private violence, armies loyal to bishops were given free reign. Tens of thousands of Christians were killed in what historians have labeled the 'Jesus wars.'

"Jesus is here today to fight religion as belief. Most of the wars in history have been fought because religion was about belief and not about a heart overflowing with love. An extreme example is the Taliban. They have made Islam into a religion of belief. When Jesus and I left the courtroom last month, he whispered to me,

'Unfortunately, we have our Taliban too.' He was referring to the church members who were hurling vicious slurs against me as we entered and left the courtroom. When I asked him later about it, he clarified the comment by saying that not all conservative Christians are Taliban-like, but there are far too many that are.

"Here's the bottom line on all this, Ellen. You don't need a scholar, a theologian, or a televangelist to define your faith. For heaven's sake, don't let a group of warring, mean-spirited, fifth-century bishops define your faith. Let God do it. Allow the experience of divine love to define it. A heart overflowing with love changes the way you see the world. The trick now becomes living according to this new perspective."

"Wow, that's a powerful statement," Ellen said as she got up from the bench. "I hate to leave you, but I need to get a quick bite to eat before the afternoon sessions. Tonight I'm going out to dinner with several of my medical-school buddies, but I can't wait to read this little book on the flight home. Thank you so much for the last hour. I will certainly get back to you."

"My home address, email, and phone number are on the last page of the book. We added a last page and printed five hundred. So here's a small stack for you to take with you. You can hand them out to friends."

"I'll do that, and I promise to get back to you soon." Jonathan stood up with her and gave her a hug.

"Have fun with you friends tonight, and thanks for being such a patient listener."

"I was enchanted. Talk to you soon," she said with a smile, and then she was on her way.

Two weeks later, Jonathan received an email from Ellen: "We need to talk. Give me a time and a day. We may need an hour." Ellen called two days later on a Sunday afternoon.

"Jonathan, it's Ellen. How are you doing?"

"Fine. What's up?"

"I've made a life-changing decision. I want to work for you. I'm giving up my practice as soon as they can find a replacement. Jeff, my husband, is fully supportive. He loved the little blue book too. We have a fourth and a second grader. I can work from home when they're at school and have more time for them when they're home."

"Fantastic. You're hired as codirector. Let me put Jesus on the line to see what he thinks."

"Oh my God. This is too much."

"Hi Ellen. This is Jesus. You're coming on board at just the right time. Jonathan can really use some help."

"I can't believe this, Jesus. I so love your message. I've already given your book away to several of my friends."

"We'll have to meet soon. I look forward to it. Here's Jonathan back."

"Jonathan, this is too much. I can't believe I just got off the phone with Jesus."

"Get used to it. Now, what do you think about being codirector?"

"On one condition. You are the up-front guy. I'm uncomfortable being the center of attention. I will be happy to do the organization work."

"We have a deal. I'm getting a little better about being up front. So, let me tell you where we are. We have $40,000 in the bank and a membership list of more than 1,500. The mail has been slowing recently, but it hasn't stopped. If you come on board, you will be in charge of the mail, the thank-you notes, and the mailing list for starters. I'm sure we'll need a newsletter soon."

"I'm on board."

"That's so nice. I'm pinching myself. The next big challenge is the website. I want you to hire a person to set up the website and manage it on a part-time basis. We need a good one, and I don't want you to worry about money. George has pledged to donate $250,000, and I have stock in a Chinese windmill company that I plan to donate to the organization. The current value of that stock is $750,000."

"Wow—that's so generous."

"I bought a million shares at five cents a share. The current price is seventy-five cents. My goal was to sell it all at two dollars a share and set up a foundation to give away the money. We now have a foundation.

"George and I both want to wait until the organization gets nonprofit status from the IRS so we don't pay taxes on our gifts. We have a lawyer friend who has a paralegal in his office who makes nonprofit applications all the time. She is doing ours on her own for $2,500, which is a steal. I gave her the little blue book to read with the hope that she will do it for free. She is also drawing up articles of incorporation."

"Wow again. I'm joining a first-class operation."

"We are making progress. As soon as we have a board of directors, I'll raise the question of a small salary for you. I know you are making a huge financial sacrifice in giving up your medical practice."

"It is a big financial sacrifice, but it's a huge gain in providing meaning in my life. My husband and I are not expecting me to receive a salary."

"That's nice, but we'll see where we are in six months. I expect we'll be in a sound position from which we can offer a small salary."

"That's certainly more than fair."

"I'll email you the mailing list as soon as we hang up and send the mail as it comes in. Prepare for a deluge. Jesus is on *Meet the Press* in two weeks."

"You guys are amazing. You're the best, Jonathan. Thank you, thank you, thank you. Now will you put Jesus back on?"

"Hi again, Ellen. Your decision to come on board has made my day."

"I love you, Jesus. You have changed my life."

7

Meet the Press

AT 8:15 ON MONDAY morning, October 18th, Dr. Julian Norcross and the associate pastor of Stillwater Baptist Church, Dr. Clinton Smithfield, left the church to head for the studio of WQHT radio, Hot 97 FM, on Hudson Street. Dr. Norcross was appearing on the *Billy Most Show* at nine. Dr. Norcross was ushered into the broadcast booth at 9:05 a.m. during an advertisement that immediately followed the local news, sports, and weather summary. Billy got up from his seat behind the microphone and a wide computer screen to shake hands with Dr. Norcross. He gestured with his left hand for Dr. Norcross to take the seat directly opposite him about six or seven feet away so that social distance was maintained. The only other person in the studio was Scott Blankenship, the technician, who sat with earphones and two computer screens directly behind Billy.

"You'll be terrific, Dr. Norcross. Just speak clearly into the mic that sits in front of you. I'll introduce you, and then we will take questions from callers around the city."

"Thirty seconds," Scott called out.

"Do you have any questions?"

"No," Dr. Norcross responded. "I have done radio interviews several times before."

"I assumed that," Billy said, "with a prominent religious leader like you. Are we all set, Scott?"

"Ready to go, boss."

"Okay. Here we go. This is Billy Most, your host for the best talk in the city. With me today is the Reverend Dr. Julian Norcross, the pastor of Stillwater Baptist Church on West Fifty-Seventh Street. Dr. Norcross, welcome."

"Thank you for having me on your show."

"There are all kinds of rumors swirling around town that Jesus has returned and that you have met him. Is that true?"

"I have met a man that goes by the name of Jesus, but he is most certainly not our Lord and Savior. I can assure you of that."

"That's why we have asked you to appear on the show. This man called Jesus is appearing on *Meet the Press* on Sunday, and we wanted to give you an opportunity to express your thoughts about him. Why are you so certain he is a fraud?"

"For one thing, he knows nothing about our sacred Scriptures."

Scott, in the background, grunted and uttered several loud ahems.

Dr. Norcross continued without missing a beat. "The book of Revelation spells out in specific detail the conditions under which our Lord will return. This imposter meets none of those conditions."

"Are you okay, Scott?" Billy asked, looking over his shoulder at his technician. "You're making a lot of noise over there."

"I didn't say anything, boss. Just attending to business."

"Just checking, old buddy. Now, Dr. Norcross, many people are not so sure about this man. It has been reported that he has done some impressive things. So, let's open the phone lines and hear from some of our good folks out there." He paused briefly before continuing. "Good morning. So, what do you think about this guy Jesus? He was good on Rosie. Is he the real deal?"

"Hi, Billy. My name is Cheryl Higgins."

A Second Chance

"Welcome to the show, Cheryl. Do you have a question for Dr. Norcross?"

"Yes, I do. I am wondering why this Jesus didn't come back to do battle with Satan."

"That's the whole point. There's nothing about this guy that fits the biblical characteristics of the Messiah. Thank you so much for your question, Cheryl. Do you have a church home? We'd love to have you worship with us at Stillwater."

"I'll give your church every consideration, Dr. Norcross."

"God bless you, Cheryl."

"Tell the jerk to pay for his advertisements," Scott whispered from behind Billy.

"My, you're feisty this morning," Billy whispered back while covering his mic. And then he looked across at Dr. Norcross. "Nice going, Dr. Norcross. Your flock seems to be growing. Our second caller is from Queens. Go ahead, please."

"Hi there, Billy. Ask the reverend if I have to get the vaccine."

"And who am I talking to?" Billy shot back.

"Roseanne Nicoletta, a 100 percent supporter of Donald J. Trump."

"Was the election stolen, Roseanne?" Billy asked.

"It certainly was, Billy. God is my witness."

"Amen to that, Roseanne. God is my witness too," Dr. Norcross interjected.

"Try putting God on the stand, you asshole," Scott whispered.

Billy spoke up quickly so as not to lose control of the interview. "Now, what about her question, Dr. Norcross? Should Roseanne get the vaccine?"

"She has every right to say no. It's her body. She has every right to control her own body."

"Then I have a question for you, Dr. Norcross," Billy said. "How does this right relate to the abortion issue? If this woman has the right to control her body with respect to the vaccine, does that include the right to have an abortion?"

"Absolutely not, Mr. Most. Abortion is murder. It violates the Ten Commandments."

"So, an unvaccinated person gives the virus to some innocent victim who ends up dying from COVID. Is that not murder?"

"No, Mr. Most. In the case of the victim you mention, that person has been called home by God."

"That wooden box is some home," Scott shot back in a whisper.

"We have another caller on the line. Loretta, also from Queens. Loretta, you're on."

"Thank you so much for having me, Billy. Like your previous caller, I love your show."

"Thank you, Loretta. We need to be hearing more from you."

"I do have a question for the preacher."

"That's why he's here."

"Ask him for me why Jesus would appoint a gay man as his messenger."

"Thank you for that question. You are right on target. Romans 1:26–28 states quite clearly that homosexuality is an abomination, an affront to God. Let me urge all of you out there to read it for yourselves."

"Speaking of sexual abominations, ask the preacher if he's still horny," Scott whispered across to Billy.

"What did you say, Scott?" Billy inquired.

"Not a thing, boss. Just focusing on our caller from Queens."

"I thought I heard you request that I ask the preacher if he is still horny," Billy said while covering the mic.

"Just attending to business, boss."

"Did you hear Scott's question, Dr. Norcross?"

Dr. Norcross spoke clearly into the mic in a deliberate, stilted voice. "I'm not sure what I heard, Mr. Most, but I can assure you our Lord would not appoint a man of the homosexual persuasion to be his messenger."

"We have another caller on the line. Candice, how are you doing this morning?"

"Fine, Billy, I'm doing fine. I love your show too. It gets my mind functioning in the morning."

"Aren't you nice. Where are you calling from?"

"Summit, New Jersey."

"What's going on in Summit?"

"Not much that's new, although my daughter just made the cheerleading squad."

"Good for her. You must be very proud. Do you have a question for our good reverend?"

"Not a question, really. I just wanted to comment that I think this guy Jesus is cute."

"Amen, sister," Scott mumbled.

Billy turned around and gave Scott the evil eye before continuing. "While we wait for another caller, Dr. Norcross, I'd love to know what you thought about the big apology at the medical convention last month."

"It was blasphemy, Mr. Most. The guy's a great deceiver. Why would Jesus want to apologize to the medical profession? To suggest that our Jesus knows nothing about the cause of disease is absurd."

"Did you disconnect my sound, Scott? I somehow lost the reverend's answer."

"That's the last straw, boys. Your technician is obviously a follower of this Satanic deceiver. I will not be a party to this deliberate attempt to contaminate our good citizens." And Dr. Norcross stormed out of the broadcast booth.

"Did you really ask that question about the preacher being horny? I can't believe it," Billy said, after pausing a minute to make sure Dr. Norcross was out of earshot and the station had gone to a commercial break.

"As I understand it from a friend, that was Jesus' question to him about a month ago at a Bible study class."

"What was he driving at?"

"It seemed to my friend that Jesus was suggesting that if Norcross was getting a little more, he might be judging a little less."

"Are you sure your friend got that right?"

"No, but if he did, Jesus' teaching puts a lot of pressure on our wives."

"I know. Mine would stop going to church."

Jesus, Jonathan, and George left on Sunday, October 24th, at seven thirty in the morning for the NBC studio at Rockefeller Plaza in the heart of Manhattan. They arrived there twenty minutes later, with plenty of time for Jesus to be touched up by the makeup artist and to receive some brief instructions for the show. In announcing the show, the spokesperson said there were two changes. The first one was that Anita Rodriguez, the religion reporter for *The New York Times*, would be standing in for Chuck Todd, the host of *Meet the Press*, who was on assignment. The second change was that the show would be broadcast from NBC's New York studio rather than the Washington bureau to accommodate both Jesus and Ms. Rodriguez.

"Good morning. My name is Anita Rodriguez, and I will be sitting in today for Chuck Todd, who is on assignment. With me this morning is Jesus. Because of the special status of our guest, I will conduct the interview without commercial breaks." Jonathan, who was sitting with George directly off from the studio, smiled as he wondered what Dr. Norcross was thinking about Jesus being described as possessing a special status. He was proud of his friend, who looked quite distinguished in his simple tunic and pleasant demeanor.

"Welcome to New York City, Jesus," Ms. Rodriguez opened with a broad smile.

"Thank you, Anita. I have really enjoyed my two months here. It's quite a change from rural Galilee."

"I was fascinated when I read about your apology to the doctors in which you admitted you had no understanding of the biological origin of disease two thousand years ago. If that is true, how do you explain your well-known reputation as a healer?"

"My reputation was inflated. When a person recovered from some malady, people talked about it and my reputation soared. When a person didn't recover, people forgot about it. What I was good at was making people feel good about themselves. As I'm sure you are aware, the mind is an important tool for healing."

"Do you have other mistakes to admit?" she asked with a laugh.

"I made many. I don't know how anyone can think of me as divine. Let me mention two big ones. I believed—and I spoke about it on numerous occasions—that God would intervene to establish his kingdom in the first century. Well, that never happened. It's quite interesting to read all the explanations from my followers as to why that has not happened. However, no matter how you look at it, it was a glaring error.

"The second big mistake is my initial understanding about how God works in the world. This one will take a little longer to explain, but it will also illustrate another point. I want all of your viewers to understand. People today know so little about the first-century me. The Gospels begin their stories when I was thirty years old, and no historians have written about my early years.

"As a result of this lack of credible historical information, people will be interested to learn I was married as a young man. There wasn't a man in my village who wasn't married. It was expected of all of us. Tragically, my wife, Anna, died giving birth to our first child. I was devasted by her death and very angry with God. I believed then in a God who controlled events in the world—the weather, the life and death of people, disease, the growth of crops, the movement of the stars, history, you name it. But now the love of my life was dead. How could a loving God who controlled events in the world allow that to happen? It's the same question Jewish victims in Nazi concentration camps asked 1,900 years later. I fled into the wilderness to escape the pain of her death. I was there for about six months.

"Slowly, the anger and my grief subsided, and once again my heart began to fill with God's love. While God had not protected my Anna, I began to awaken each morning with the sense that life was good, that the love from God was real. The wildflowers and streams were speaking to me again. From this experience, I came to conclude that the operation of God in the world was more subtle than I had assumed. God withdraws from direct control to allow humans to possess free will, but her love and compassion for us is ever present. I wish now I had done a better job conveying this insight in the first century."

"That's fascinating, Jesus. Your description fits my God to a tee. Let me now change the subject and ask: You have been in this country for a little more than two months. What worries you about us?"

"I was expecting that question and thought about my answer on the way over here. There are three things that worry me about your country. The first is guns. So many Americans own them, and many of those who do claim to be my followers. Can't they read? I admit that not all the stories about me in the New Testament are totally accurate, but the Gospel writers got my teachings on nonviolence correct.

"I will also admit that it is hard for humans to be pacifists, though not impossible. It is built into instinctive human behavior, our reptilian heritage, to defend ourselves. But gun ownership in America is ridiculous. The violence that results is disgusting and so unnecessary.

"Can I go a little philosophical on you?" Jesus asked with a smile. He answered his own question by continuing. "Two important societal values clash over this issue. The first one is individual freedom. We had little sense of this value in first-century Palestine, much to our detriment. The United States has been a beacon for the world in promoting this value. You should be proud of your legacy in this regard.

"On the other hand, there is the value of community, the collective good, the needs and rights of the larger society. This is the value that is central to my teachings. Humans are the most dependent animals in God's kingdom. You see it best in our first years and toward the end of life, but this dependency is always present. We need each other. Individuals benefit when the rights of the larger group are taken into consideration.

"We need to balance the two values to maintain a well-functioning society. The problem is that there are some people in your society who have taken the freedom value to extremes. They oppose any form of gun control. They believe they have an absolute right to own a gun of any make or type. The result: thousands die each year from runaway gun violence. No other country in the developed world has this problem. Many of these self-centered freedom extremists also oppose vaccine mandates. 'No government has the right to tell me what to do with my body,' they say. The result: thousands of unnecessary deaths have occurred from the COVID pandemic because of their inability to see the needs and rights of the community. Balance is a good thing. Aristotle said that long before my time.

"That was a long-winded answer, and I need to get back to your question. I also worry about climate change. It's happening, it's preventable, and it's destroying the planet. The cause is human greed. People clamor for more and more things. The central belief of so many people is that unrestrained economic growth is a good thing—the more growth, the better.

"Make no mistake about it. This is a Christian issue. Day after day, I spoke about the joy of simple living. There are two billion Christians in the world today who claim to be followers of me, and yet the vast majority of them ignore these teachings on simple living. They clamor for more and more. Your consumer-driven economy has created a numbing denial of the problem. Maybe the recent hurricanes, floods, and wildfires will wake people up. I hope so. In the meantime, it's a huge disappointment, and it's destroying our precious planet, as I said at the outset.

"And the third is economic equality. This value lies at the core of your founding documents. Let's do it! The economy has never been so skewed in favor of the rich in your country. It's time to right that injustice."

"Can you tell me how? What would you recommend we do to remedy this problem?"

"The first thing I would say is that you need to make major changes, but not revolutionary change. Revolutions in history have so often turned out badly, with thousands losing their lives and an unjust, authoritarian system replacing the corrupt old system.

"Private ownership has led to many good things. It has created impressive economic wealth which has allowed literally millions of people around the globe to move out of poverty. That is also true in your country; however, many have been left behind. The ones left behind are the ones I'm concerned about.

"To give the have-nots lives of meaning and purpose with economic security, your country needs to make large investments in education, job training, low-cost housing, and health care. A great deal more economic support needs to go to the mentally ill and handicapped. They are children of God, too, and need to be treated as such.

"Such investments will be expensive, and the question becomes that of how you will pay for them. The answer for me is quite simple. The money will come from two sources—increased taxes on the rich and reduced military spending.

"The wealthy think they have achieved their economic success on their own, by their own hard work and ingenuity. The truth is they have had lots of help from a supporting society. They could not have done it without good teachers, a supportive economic infrastructure, and a home environment that was safe and secure. In many ways, the wealthy have benefited most from American society, and it's time they give back.

"With regard to military spending, you are obsessed with military security. You have bases all over the world, and you spend on defense more than the next ten countries in line put together. Your expenditures are geared for empire rather than homeland security. If you want to have a positive influence in the world, send vaccines, not troops. Show by example that you can feed the poor, house the homeless, provide health care for all of your citizens. You could cut your military spending by half and the sun would rise in the morning, and most Americans would never know the difference."

"Those are blunt, honest answers. Can we now look at the glass as half full? Tell us what you admire most about our country."

"You are quite unique in the world in that you were founded on an idea, not membership in a tribe or racial identity or religious belief. Your founding fathers clearly stated in your foundation documents that all humans are created equal and with that status come certain rights. That is God's vision for human governance. That is my vision. I preached day after day in the first century about the importance of inclusion. I shared meals with all different kinds of people my enemies labeled as sinners. Your country is a multiracial democracy. It's a beautiful ideal. Keep working at it."

"You spoke a while back about people who are refusing to get the vaccine. Many of those people are conservative Christians who are skeptical of modern science. The question of the relationship between religion and science is a big one. Can you enlighten us on that topic?"

"I can try. As I see it, there is no conflict between religion and science. They look at the world differently, with different goals. Science has a narrow focus, looking objectively at what is out there to solve a concrete problem. This focus has provided many benefits—the cell phone, which I now have in my possession." He smiles into the camera. "Science has cured many diseases; humans are living far longer. It has provided us with inexpensive solar panels, and the list goes on and on. Science is also certainly correct with its diagnosis of the problems relating to climate change and the COVID pandemic.

"The one thing science can't do is come up with a complete understanding of reality itself. Some scientists try, but they keep changing their theories. The truth is that ultimate reality is so much greater than any scientific theory can construct. The deeper we look into the center of reality, the more mysterious it gets. It is here that religion takes over. It fashions a human response to the deep mystery, beauty, and goodness of the universe."

"I really like that answer, but I'm afraid we must change the subject again," she said while smiling broadly at her guest. "There is just so much to cover, and we only have an hour. The State of Texas recently passed a very restrictive law making it almost impossible for a woman in the state to obtain an abortion. Can you speak to that issue?"

"Oh dear. Do I have to?" Jesus responded, smiling.

"I don't want to put you in a difficult position. We can move on to another question."

"No, I came here to answer all of your questions, and this one provides me with an opportunity to make a point about how God works in the world. There will be viewers who won't like what I have to say about abortion. The one thing I will tell them is this: when I speak about abortion, it is not God speaking. God's voice is always difficult to discern, because it is filtered through a human personality which has its own agenda and biases. The best way to discern God's voice is when your heart is overflowing with love. Pay attention to subtle messages that float through your awareness when your heart is full. In all probability, God is speaking. Messages that float through your awareness when you are coping with the day-to-day or anger are most likely not from God.

"Now to answer your question. On the one hand, every person is the captain of the ship when it comes to the functioning of their body. A man might justifiably be angry if a group of women said he could not have a vasectomy because it violated the will of God by restricting procreation.

"On the other hand, abortion is a disgusting form of birth control. Let me repeat that. Abortion is a disgusting form of birth control.

"So, what should we do about it? The two sides should work together to limit the use of abortion as a tool of birth control. Wouldn't that be nice for the two sides to work together! Both sides have a common interest in adoption. We need to remove the bureaucratic hurdles that make adoption such a difficult process. We also need to provide counseling to the pregnant woman and her partner. They should be told that bringing a healthy baby into the world is a great gift. The woman should be provided with all the health care services needed to achieve a healthy birth. Toward the end of her pregnancy, discussion should commence regarding the responsibilities of parenting. If the couple is unable or unwilling to assume those responsibilities, the woman should be counseled to offer up her child for adoption.

"Let me make one final point. Many of my followers love the fetus in utero but abandon the baby once the birth takes place. Over the last several years, they have dramatically reduced government spending for childcare services. If you don't intend to provide services to indigent parents to allow their children adequate health care, nutrition, and schooling, it would be better for the child not to have been born."

"Your answer sounds like God speaking to me."

"Be careful with that, Anita. You are only asking for your hate mail to increase. One of the clearest indicators that religion in my name has become a failure is the lack of civility practiced by politicians who jump to the microphone claiming to be Christian and then go on to demean an opponent unfairly. You see it on both sides."

"Moving away from politics, let me ask you about the state of Christianity in America. Polling over the last several years has shone a rather discouraging decline in church membership among Americans. Do you have any ideas to explain why this is happening?"

"As I understand it, most of the decline comes from young people, which is not difficult to understand. When churches preach salvation in heaven, young kids look up at the sky and ask where this place is the preacher is talking about. They wonder how God impregnated my mother. They wonder why, if I walked the earth after being crucified, no first-century historian wrote about this amazing occurrence. They wonder why the accounts of my physical resurrection in the Gospels all differ. The Gospels don't even agree as to where I met my disciples after dying on the cross.

"If churches were about saving the world and not about the salvation of individual souls and all that silly dogma I just referred to, churches would fill again. People want to be a part of a loving community. Many want a more just and less violent society. They want an institution that stands for what is best in the world."

"What about life after death? I mean, here you are—back with us."

"I'm not going to answer that question, because I want you and everyone out there listening to live to the fullest extent now. I want you to live lives of joy, creativity, and meaning while at the same time living the love that God so graciously places in your hearts. Life is filled with mystery, and the question of what happens when we die is the last question for which we will receive an answer. I will say this, however. If there is an afterlife, it's not reserved for people who believe in me. It will be open to all people, because the essence of God is love. A God of love would not exclude people from different religious backgrounds."

"A few minutes ago, I asked you what worried you about America. Let me ask you now if you have any concerns about religion."

"I worry greatly about the disconnect between religion and nature that is occurring as the world becomes more secular. God created the earth, and as a result, that is where God is known. God is sensed when you stare at wildflowers, marvel when gazing at a mountaintop, swim in the clear blue water of a rushing river, walk in fresh snow. More and more humans are living in a world of their own creation—a virtual reality with all their devices, their elaborate houses which insulate them from God's world and isolate them from their neighbors.

"For nine months out of the year, I slept on a flat roof and gazed at the stars. I sat and marveled at wildflowers, swam in beautiful streams. We didn't have cell phones, personal computers, and all the other consumer devices that allow humans to live in a world of their own creation. The result is that religion today is all about human-created belief. It is not about sensing the deep love of God and the essential goodness of life which comes from living in God's world."

"Is that why you came back now—to preach this message about religion? I admit it's a unique message. I have never thought about the problem of leaving God's world for a world of my own creation."

"That's a really good question, and it's right on target. The world is currently on an unsustainable path. The window for dealing with climate change is closing, the increased possession of nuclear weapons is scary, the rise in economic inequality is unprecedented. What I'm saying is that if you have a real sense of God in your heart, that if you know God in some experiential way, you could never condone the possession of nuclear weapons. What I am saying is that if you lived in God's world, that if you experienced the natural world in a deep way, it would break your heart to see the world being ruined because of the excessive greed of humans that is causing temperatures to rise.

"Religion as ideology, as belief, doesn't touch your heart. You can do atrocious things if it supports your ideology. Just look at the Taliban—an extreme example, I admit. If you believe as the central focus of your religion in God guaranteeing you a place in heaven, why limit your consumption to save the climate? You're going to a better place. This fast-paced, device-driven world squeezes God from our awareness.

"So, I'm here to tell people that there is a second chance. This may sound arrogant, but I believe my teachings are still relevant. Simple living, inclusion, a focus on economic and social justice, and the practice of nonviolence will make the world a far better place. We need to know God, not believe in him."

"Wow, Jesus, that is some message. It saddens me to say that we are running out of time. In the minute we have left, can you fill us in on your plans for the immediate future?"

"I plan to be leaving the United States within the week, Anita. I have had a fabulous two months here. I have an archeology friend in Israel who is currently on a dig in Magdala, the home of my great friend Mary. He called me the other day to say they are getting close to uncovering the first century. I would love to see if we can find the foundation of Mary's house. Her family had a fish-salting business. The family shared their profits with us to help fund our movement in the first century. I would love to find evidence of that. I guess you could say I'm a sentimental guy."

"I would say you are far more than that. Thank you so much for spending this time with us. For regular viewers, Chuck Todd will be back next Sunday with his usual cast of movers and shakers in Washington. For viewers interested in finding out more about this new Jesus movement, please stay on the air. We will flash all the necessary contact information for you. As for me, it has been my greatest honor to do this interview. Thank you so much, NBC News, for giving me this opportunity. And again, thank you, Jesus of Nazareth, for sharing this time with us."

8

The Last Supper

"I WANT TO WELCOME you all to our home," Jonathan said as he smiled broadly at his friends around the table. "Jesus asked if we could have a dinner together so that he could thank all of you for what you have done to get our organization started and running. For the first time in a long while, I'd like to start this meal with grace. Jesus, would you do us the honor of saying grace?"

"Let us pray. Heavenly Father and Mother, bless these good friends sitting here at your table. They have taken such good care of me over the last two months, and I will surely miss them as I resume my travels. They are living proof that humans are indeed created in your image. And with that said, I ask that you bless this food to our use, and us to your faithful service. Amen."

"Is this the last supper? Are you leaving us?" George asked.

"Yes, I am leaving tomorrow afternoon, but I hate to call this the 'last supper,' because some New Testament writers have distorted the meaning of that wonderful meal. Most Christians associate the Last Supper with sin. My purpose on earth was never to serve as a sacrifice for sin. God is not that petty. A God who really loves her people wouldn't require me to die as a condition for Christians to be saved. The Last Supper I had with my disciples was a meal to celebrate Passover. So, let's celebrate!"

"I'm celebrating being home again," Jonathan said, rising from his chair. "I've been away for almost a week signing on with an agent to organize a concert tour and a host of other events. I'm glad to be back home with friends. I also really missed George. On one especially lonely night, I wrote a song about living with George called 'Here.'

"You can get arrested for writing about that stuff. I'd be careful, Queenie," George responded with a laugh.

"Well, if you all won't rat on me, I'd like to play it for you. While I'm doing that, you can take the two little boys to the kitchen to help serve up the main course."

Here

We've been together so long
You are my friend and lover
Another season goes on
When we're together,
When we're together

Here.
Living with you right here
All through the years
Here
Living with you right here
All through the years.

We've built a good foundation
We wish each other happiness
No need for explanation
When we're together
When we're together

Here.
Living with you right here
All through the years.

I promise to be there when the sun doesn't shine
Through sickness and sorrow.
You've given me your heart, and I've given you mine
Today and tomorrow
In staring at the future, I see in your eyes
I see it's forever.

Here.
Living with you right here
All through the years
Here
Living with you right here
All through the years.

"Nice song, Queenie," Brad said. "Who cooked the beef, Wellington? It's fantastic too."

"I did," Jonathan replied. "It's fun to be back in the kitchen again. Bon appétit, everyone, and while we're having dinner, it would be fitting of the occasion for each one of you, beginning with Rebecca, to describe briefly what you have to celebrate."

"With you leaving us, Jesus, I doubt very much we will ever play the scripture-challenge game again. So before you go, I would like to ask if you have anything to add to Paul's famous statement that all are one in Christ—male/female, Jew/Gentile, and slave/free."

"I would hope Paul would now be able to add 'gay/straight.'"

"I suspected that would be your response. I just have to say that Ron and I are so grateful for your coming back to affirm our dear friends."

"We are all God's children, Rebecca," Jesus said, smiling across at her.

"Thank you so much for that," Rebecca said, returning his smile.

"Okay, you're up next, Brad," Jonathan said.

"Greg and I are grateful for having the opportunity to meet you, Jesus. You have inspired us. We think you're the real deal. We have made a small contribution to the organization and look forward to receiving marching orders from Ellen with regard to how we can help in the future."

"Be careful what you promise, Brad," George said. "I can see from here that Ellen is making mental notes."

"We will certainly find things for you guys to do. I want to thank you all for inviting my family to come here to meet Jesus. It will be an experience my little boys, especially, will never forget."

"At least he didn't come down a chimney," George called out.

"I love you, George," Jesus said. "You're also impossible—worse than the Pharisees."

"But you bested them."

"I know, but I can't best you. You are the best," Jesus said, laughing.

"Don't make me a sinner, Jesus. You're stoking my pride."

"Okay, I'll back off and give the floor back to Ellen."

"Wow—you boys are a hard act to follow. Starting again, thank you, Jonathan and George, for inviting us all here. I'm thrilled Jeff is here to meet you all. I've never had more work to do, so it's good that he sees for himself what I've been telling him, that this movement could change the world.

"Jesus, you hit a home run on *Meet the Press*. The mail is in boxes, the email is off the menu page, and the phone is off the hook. We are looking to hire three employees and have found a small but comfortable office to rent in Pittsburgh. As I just said, Jesus, I have never worked so hard, and I have never had such fulfilling work to do." And she burst into tears. "I just can't believe all these good things are happening to me and my family. Let me end by saying I have acquired a second father with Jonathan."

"I'm sorry about all that mail, Ellen," Jesus said, smiling across at her. "I guess it will keep you busy for a while. I can't tell you how good I feel with you in charge of all the administrative details surrounding our new movement. Jeff, you married a gem of a woman."

"I'm a lucky man, Jesus," Jeff interjected, smiling across at his wife.

"I've spoken out of turn a few times, but I just would like to add: Jesus, you have changed Queenie's life. I've never seen him more energized or happy. You have also inspired a guy who before you invaded our lives couldn't give a rat's ass about religion. That's quite an accomplishment, sir. Let me end by saying that yes, you are leaving tomorrow afternoon, but it better not be the last time we see you."

"I have good news for you, George," Jonathan said. "We have plans to meet at least once a year. As with Ellen, I have never worked harder in my life, but I have found God again. Working for this wonderful movement has been life transforming. I just hope we can deliver for you, Jesus."

"You already have, Jonathan. I can't believe our organization has achieved this much in such a short time. Here is what I am grateful for, and it runs deep. Religion in my name has been failing. Christians have distorted my message and created their own religion around the myth of personal salvation in heaven. It's not easy to face the fact that your life's work is turning into a failure, but you wonderful folks are going to save me by redefining Christianity according to my original message in the first century. The people sitting around this table are going to make me a winner. God bless you! From the deepest recesses of my heart, God bless you!"